"Socks, or stockings, if you prefer, are an essential part of my business model, so I'm always happy to see them celebrated in literature. "Sockworld" is the perfect stocking stuffer."   --S. Claus

"My name is Socks, and this is my world, so, like, do I get royalties?" -- Socks the cat

**"This book is Greek to me."
- Sockrates**

SOCKWORLD

SOCKWORLD
by Cary Grossman

KALLISTO GAIA
PRESS

for
Anthony

1

All day at school Purdy's mind flew around above his head like a bird on a leash. He had a new story simmering, and he knew the only way to stop thinking about it was to write it down. As soon as he got home, he set right to work.

In walked trouble. C.B. was standing in the candy aisle of a mini-mart and could see it right away. Two young punks came through the door with shifty eyes and long jackets. "Who wears long jackets in the desert in summer?" C.B. thought. One punk stopped to look at the magazines in the front of the store. The other came down the candy aisle. As he zipped past C.B. the punk's jacket flew open and C.B. could see a gun tucked in his pants. The punk with the gun went all the way to the back of the store then started up the next aisle. Over the shelves he swapped glances with the other punk, then took the gun out. Sudden-ly a giant purple claw reached down from the ceiling, clamped onto the gun and yanked it out of his hand. "What the..." said the punk, and then his eyes opened wide. "Crab Boy!" The giant claw smashed into his face and down he went.

Purdy put down his pencil and re-read what he had just written. The part about the candy reminded him that he didn't have his usual snack when he got home. He reached into the backpack beneath his desk. His hand crawled through the dark, crowded interior and emerged at last bearing a limp candy bar that had been smashed flat by his heavy 7th grade math book. Once he had poured all the broken bits of candy into his mouth he returned to reading. He paused again when he got to the part about the purple claw, and glanced up at the clear plastic box on his desk where a small hermit crab was poking at a cube of dried fruit with its own purple claw.

"Hey, Claw Machine," Purdy said, "you're a superhero." Like millions of other boys, and perhaps a few dozen girls, Purdy had always wanted to be a superhero himself. All his favorite movies, TV shows, and video games seemed to point to superhero as the ideal career. He found, however, there were consid-erable obstacles to achieving this goal. The first and most obvious roadblock to his becoming a superhero was the fact that he had no superpowers. He wasn't especially strong or fast, his eyesight and hearing just average. He was bright, but that only served to make him bored with school. His only weapon—the occasional witty remark; his only defense—the protective space he maintained between himself and others, for reasons he himself did not entirely understand.

In addition to his lack of superpowers, Purdy felt disadvantaged by not being an orphan. All the great superheroes—Superman, Batman, Spiderman— were orphans. Purdy was, at best, only half an orphan because his father disappeared when he was three. He loved his mother and could not imagine getting along without her. Still, she was a drawback.

Finally, Purdy was appalled to live in a trailer park on the edge of a small town in southern Arizona. Everyone knows superheroes live in big cities. Yes, Superman grew up in the country, but he didn't stay there, preventing tractor accidents, and protecting cows from getting tipped over by bored teenagers. There aren't enough evil, demented scum in a small town to keep a superhero busy for a half hour. To be a superhero you have to live in a big city where the supply of evil, demented scum is limitless.

Even when very young Purdy didn't believe superheroes really existed, though he ardently wished they did. Having accepted it was all a game he enjoyed applying the rules of logic to their illogical world. "Batman couldn't possibly be strong enough to pick that bad guy off the ground with one hand," he would reason, "so his suit must be equipped with hydraulics." To compensate for his inability to become a superhero, Purdy liked to write stories about superheroes and, for a while, lived vicariously through the adventures of Captain Gas or Crab Boy.

"Knock, knock. Hi darlin'." Purdy's mother, Doreen, appeared in the doorway of his bedroom, sipping on a can of beer and leafing through a handful of mail. She had not yet changed out of her supermarket uniform, a white shirt and khaki pants, but her feet were bare. "How was school?" she asked, her speech still shaded by the Appalachian Mountains of her childhood.

"It was there," said Purdy. "How was work?"

"There," Doreen said. "What are you up to?"

"Writing a story."

"Well that's nice, but couldn't you do that later? I wish you'd get outside more and blow the stink off you. Aren't there any boys you can play with?"

Purdy shook his head. "The boys in this town are all morons."

"Oh. Well, I didn't say you had to play chess with them. How about the girls?"

His mother's raised eyebrow told him he'd better be careful with his answer. "And the girls…" Purdy said, "are all too smart to mess with me."

His mother laughed. "Well, at least that much will change. Once they get to be teenagers girls get a good sight dumber about boys. Besides, you're good looking."

"You have to say that because you're my mother."

"No, I don't have to say it 'cause I'm your mother. I have to say it 'cause you look like me."

Purdy's mother did, in fact, look quite a bit like him, the same red hair and green eyes, but where Purdy's countenance was generally closed and suspicious, Doreen nearly always looked to be on the verge of giggling. Adult faces are of two sorts. When you look at some adults you see ahead to what they will look like when they become old, see where the skin will sag and eyes will sink, where all the little lines will deepen and set. The faces of other adults point backwards. You can clearly see what they looked like when they were young children, detect, beneath the façade of maturity, youthful anxiety, and glee. Doreen Hooper's face fell into the latter category. Looking at her you could easily imagine her as a child, running through the forests with her sister and cousins, or watching with hushed expectation as her father made a show of lighting the Christmas tree for the first time.

When his mother had left the room Purdy returned to writing his latest adventure.

The other punk came around the corner. "Crab Boy!" he said, and pulled out his gun. "You know what? I hate seafood."

"Well," said Crab Boy, "I hate greasy, gun-toting slime burgers like you. Does that make us even?"

The punk started shooting. With super speed, Crab Boy's giant claw flicked away all the bullets – Ping! Ping! Ping! When the punk's gun was empty he threw it and ran. Before he reached the door Crab Boy's giant claw grabbed the back of his jacket and tossed him into the air so forcefully the punk's head got stuck in the ceiling.

"Clean up on aisle nine," said Crab Boy.

"It's a good story," said a voice.

"Thanks," said Purdy. Then, startled, he sat straight up. He looked for a moment at his pet crab, and then swiveled in his chair, looking all around the room. "Who said that?"

There were a few moments of silence and then the voice spoke again. "You can hear me?"

"Yes, I can hear you," said Purdy, standing up now, and shaking a bit. "Who are you? Where are you?" All he heard in response was the sound of muffled sobbing.

<>

2

Purdy **inched toward his bed.** He reached out, grasped the blanket hanging to the floor, flung it up onto the bed, and jumped back. He crouched down and peered under the bed. There was no one under there. He looked around and picked up a long stick with a plastic shark's head at the tip which he won at the State Fair. He slowly approached his open closet and, with sudden ferocity, poked the shark again and again into the hanging clothes. No one was in the closet. He leapt at his window and threw aside the curtains. Outside a startled quail flew up from the gravel path with a gurgled cry. No one was outside. Purdy was satisfied that he was alone in his room yet still he heard the quiet crying. "This is not funny," he said. "I'm going to call the police."

"I'm sorry," said the voice, a man's voice. "It's been so long since anyone could hear me." Another sob. "I didn't, I didn't think you ever would."

Purdy called, "Mom!"

"I don't think she can hear me," said the voice. "I've tried."

"Mama!" Purdy yelled.

"What is it?" said Doreen as she bounded through the door with a shoe in her hand. "A roach? A spider?"

"No, no," said Purdy. "I keep hearing a voice. Listen." They listened.

"Well, say something!" Purdy commanded.

"What should I say?" said the voice.

"There," said Purdy. "Did you hear that?"

"I didn't hear nothing," said Doreen.

"Louder," said Purdy.

The voice started singing:

> *"Little tomato, hangin' on the vine,*
> *If I pick you will you be mine?*
> *Little tomato, hangin' on the vine.*
> *You know that I love you —*
> *Please be my Valentine."*

"You hear that?" said Purdy. "He's singing now."

"Ah," said Doreen. She walked around the small room, straining to hear.

> *"So red and so ready, little tomater,*
> *If it ain't now it surely will be later.*
> *Little tomato, catch up if you can.*
> *You know that I love you —*

5

Please let me be your man."

"You hear it?" said Purdy.

"No." Doreen looked at her son, and then tapped her chin to indicate she had an idea. "You know, I heard once that sometimes the metal fillings in people's teeth can pick up radio signals. Maybe that's what you hear. Open your mouth -- let me listen."

Purdy opened his mouth and his mother bent to put her ear beside it. Then she reached up, grabbed Purdy's ear, and twisted it.

"Ouch!" said Purdy. "What are you doing?"

"I'm trying to change the station," she said, and fell back laughing.

"This is not funny," Purdy insisted.

"Sorry, Darlin', I didn't hear nothing." She tousled his hair. "Don't worry. It's probably the neighbor's TV or radio. You know how sound bounces around these old tin cans. I've got supper in the oven." She left the room.

"I told you she wouldn't hear me," said the voice.

"Shut up!" said Purdy.

As if obeying the request, the voice fell silent, and Purdy did not attempt speaking to it. He felt he would be happy if he never heard it again. A short time later, his mother called him to dinner. He ate his chicken nuggets and macaroni and cheese in silence, his eyes focused on the plate in front of him, hardly ever looking up at the TV.

"Everything OK in school?" asked Doreen.

"Huh?"

"Anything bothering you?"

"Oh, no, everything's fine," said Purdy. "Why?"

"You've been stirring that mac and cheese for five minutes. You want something else?"

"No, everything's good," he said, eating several forkfuls to prove the point. He could not tell her that he had spent the last ten minutes trying to decide if he was losing his mind. He knew that crazy people often heard voices. Try as he might he couldn't come up with a more reasonable explanation for the voice. He toyed with the idea that someone had hidden a speaker in his room to play a prank on him, but though he was sometimes pranked at school he knew there was no one who liked him enough to follow him home and prank him. He couldn't even think of anyone who disliked him enough to do it. He had his share of bullies at school but they were garden variety jerks who would knock the books out from under his arm, or shove him into the lockers, or punch him when no one was looking. None with the imagination or intelligence for such an elaborate prank. No, crazy seemed the likeliest explanation.

"And what if I am?" he reasoned. *"It's not my fault. It's a chemical thing. I'll just have to get some medicine and I'll be fine."*

"Mom?" he said. "Has anyone in our family ever been crazy?"

"On my side of the family or your daddies?" said Doreen.

"Both, I guess."

"Oh Lord yes!" said Doreen.

Purdy sighed. After dinner Purdy announced that he was going to take a walk to the Stop 'N' Shop to get medicine. When he said "medicine" both he and his mother knew he meant candy. For as long as he could remember Purdy had experienced brief dizzy spells. They came and went quickly, for no apparent reason. Recently Purdy had found he could even bring them on himself by shutting his eyes and concentrating on a spot in the middle of his forehead where they seemed to start. He didn't tell his mother he had dizzy spells until he was eight, because he had assumed everyone had them. She took him to the doctor, who ran some tests but couldn't find anything wrong with him.

The doctor suggested that perhaps during the day Purdy had episodes of low blood sugar, so whenever he felt dizzy he should drink a glass of orange juice or eat a piece of candy. This was, Purdy thought, the most brilliant prescription he ever heard of. The doctor might just as easily have said he needed a shot, or some nasty tasting medicine, or more vegetables. Instead he gave Purdy permission to eat more candy. Ever since that time Purdy had the highest regard for doctors, even though it appeared to him that they were only guessing most of the time.

"Walking to the store?" said Doreen. "You never walk. You always ride your bike."

"I know," said Purdy, "but I feel like walking."

"OK. Be careful. Get home before dark." It was 5:30 in the evening but it was early September so it would remain light out for more than an hour.

As Purdy closed the front door behind him the voice said, "I'll go along with you."

<>

3

*E*arly evening in the small town of Casi Nada, Arizona, is not exactly quiet. Always, somewhere, a radio is blaring a Mexican or Rap station. Always, somewhere, there is a dog barking. There are usually children screaming. At 6:00 the church bells chime. Birds crowd into the trees and argue before settling down for the night. Most of the year there are thousands of crickets, all singing, "Be My Love." All the noise, however, could not drown out the voice in Purdy's head.

"I'm sure you have questions," said the voice.

Purdy walked on a few steps more, then stopped and took a deep breath.

"Are you God?" he asked.

"What?" said the voice.

"Are you God? If you are, I'm sorry for telling you to shut up. Am I going to have to climb up some mountain, like, um, what's his name? Sorry, they kicked me out of Sunday School when I was five for asking too many hard questions. I seem to remember God was always sending people up mountains."

The voice laughed. "No, I'm definitely not God."

"OK," said Purdy, and considered his next question. "Are you the devil?"

"The devil? When did you get so religious?"

"When you hear voices in your head you are either religious or crazy. If you don't mind, I'd rather be religious."

"I am not the devil," said the voice, "and you are not crazy."

Purdy began walking again. "That's just what the devil would say."

"Listen," said the voice, "I'm just a regular person, just like you."

"Sure, mister, just like me," said Purdy, "except you're invisible and only I can hear you."

"OK, Purdy," said the voice, "why don't you stop walking for a minute and I'll try to explain."

Purdy would have stopped walking anyway, momentarily shocked to hear the voice call him by his name. "You know my name, but I don't know yours."

"Oh, yes," said the voice. "Well, hmm, why don't you call me Joe?"

Purdy leaned up against a light pole. "What do you mean, 'call me Joe?' Is that your name or isn't it?"

"Um, no, not exactly. It's complicated."

"No, no," said Purdy, "it's simple. I can just assume that everything you tell me is a lie."

"No," said Joe. "I'll tell you when I'm lying."

"Oh, gee, thanks."

"OK," said Joe, "I'll try my best to explain everything, but it won't be easy. I don't understand it all myself. Do you hear that radio?" There was a radio playing in the distance. "You know that all around you, and even going right through you, there are radio waves, right? Even though you can't see or feel them? The world is just like that. There is the part you can see and hear and touch, and then there are other layers that you can't really sense, but that are just as real, like radio waves, or like the kind of sounds dogs can hear but you can't, or ultraviolet light, or radiation, or, um, what are those particles called? Neutrinos. With me so far?"

Purdy nodded and said, "I guess."

"Well," Joe continued, "some years ago – I don't know how – I slipped into a different layer of the world. Not one of those alternate universes you hear so much about. It's very much your world, but it doesn't touch it somehow. It's like a layer of the world just made of energy, or images, or something. I still look like myself, but I don't have a physical body. I can float around, move in any direction, as fast as I want. I don't feel anything. I can pass right through walls, and trees, and even you. I don't eat, or drink, or breathe. I'm like a hologram, you know, like a 3-D image."

Purdy inhaled sharply and started walking, walking fast. "Joe," he said, "I'm sorry to break this to you, but you're dead."

"No, I'm not."

"Look it up. Don't eat, don't drink, don't breathe – that means you're dead."

"I'm not."

"You're a ghost, mister. I'm really sorry. Go into the light."

"Purdy, I really don't think I'm dead. I'll tell you why. A few months ago there was this stupid little poodle in here that kept following me around. For weeks I couldn't get rid of him, and then one day he somehow popped back into your world. He seemed just fine, perfectly healthy. Somebody picked him up and fed him and took him to the pound, I imagine, as I haven't seen him around. By now he's probably adopted and annoying someone else. So, I think I'm still alive, just in a different form. You know everything in the universe is made of energy, and energy is always changing forms. One day it's a star, one day, a billion years later, it's a parakeet. Solid, liquid, gas – just different forms of the same stuff."

"Huh!" said Purdy. "So why don't you pop back out here?"

"Oh, God, I've tried. I've tried every day for years. I don't know how."

As Purdy was walking past a house, a pit bull that had been sleeping by the front door got up, barked, and ran toward him.

"Hello Beans," said Purdy. The dog started wagging its tail, wagging its whole back end as it came to greet him. "Who's a good boy? Who's a good boy?" Purdy rubbed the dog's big round head with his knuckles and told him he'd see him later.

"So," said Purdy, "is there anyone else in there with you, besides poodles?"

"Oh, it's hardly crowded. You run into other people now and then. No one you'd want to hang out with. A few animals get stuck in here. I feel really bad for them. They don't understand. They float around all depressed. And there are a lot of socks floating around."

"Socks?"

"Yeah, weird, huh? I guess all the socks that get lost in the wash end up here."

Purdy arrived in front of the Stop 'N' Shop. The new owner, Amar, was outside winding up the striped awning with a long metal pole. "Hey, how you doing?" Amar said.

"Howdy," said Purdy. "Doing good."

"Good, good. Go in. I'll be in in a minute."

Purdy went straight back to the candy section. "He's always trying to sell me fruit," he said to Joe. He tried to decide between chocolate and something so sour that he'd have to make funny faces to eat it. "How come you don't want to hang out with the other people in Sockworld? Are you anti-social or something?"

"No," said Joe. "It's just most everyone here has been here for years and years, and it's like being in prison, like being in solitary confinement. It drives you nuts after a while."

"Oh. So how long did you say you've been in there?"

The bell on the door tinkled and Amar came inside, so Purdy had to stop talking. He brought a candy bar up to the front counter and tried not to stare too much at Amar's ears, which had the longest drooping earlobes Purdy had ever seen.

"Ah, more candy," said Amar. "How about a nice orange instead? It's sweet as sugar, I promise. I had one for lunch."

"Maybe another time," said Purdy, counting out seventy-five cents in nickels and dimes.

"Thank you," said Amar. "Take care."

Once outside, Purdy could talk again. "What I don't get is why I can hear you."

"I've tried talking to thousands of people," said Joe. "You're the first to hear me. I don't know. I guess we have a connection."

"Lucky me," said Purdy.

"No, lucky me. You can't imagine how nice it is to talk to someone.

Maybe you can help me figure out how to get out of here."

"Me? I'm just a kid."

"But you're smart. You can study up, read books. If I could I'd read about physics, but I can only read over people's shoulders. I can see books but can't touch them. But you can."

"Oh, yeah, sure. Look, how about I get a college degree in physics and get back to you in about fifteen years?"

As Purdy approached the trailer park where he lived he slowed to a stop. "Where are you now, exactly?"

"I'm right in front of you," said Joe. Purdy put his hands out. "There," said Joe, "you just put your hand right through me."

"I didn't feel anything."

"Neither did I."

"But you can see me?" Purdy said.

"Perfectly well."

"And if I'm in the bathroom or the shower?"

"No," said Joe. "I respect your privacy. I know your pre-teen imagination thinks being invisible is good for only one thing – seeing people naked. Trust me, that gets old real fast."

Purdy thought for a moment. "Have you seen my mom naked?"

"No."

"You're lying, right?"

"Yes. Really, seeing naked people is not the big deal you think it is."

"But you're not going to do it anymore, right?"

"Right."

"OK Joe, I need you to leave me for a while. I mean I don't mind talking to you, but I don't think I can stand to have your voice in my head 24/7."

"No, you're right," said Joe. "I get that. You need your space. I'll still visit you now and then, like a friend dropping by, but I'll stay away when you're busy, or naked."

"Thanks."

Purdy climbed the steps to his front door, then turned back. "You know, I didn't really think you were God," he said.
"Why not?"

"I don't think God cries like a three-year-old girl."

"Ah," said Joe. "Maybe not. Good night."

Although he didn't hear Joe's voice again that evening, his new invisible acquaintance was hardly out of Purdy's mind, and he could not sleep most of the night because the conversation he had with Joe kept playing over in his head.

4

Purdy's nose was nodding closer and closer to the papers on his desk when a knock on the classroom door woke him. His teacher, Mrs. Martinez, opened the door and said, "Come in, dear." She ushered in a girl with long black hair.

"Class," said Mrs. Martinez, "we have a new student joining us today." She went to the white board and spoke slowly as she wrote the girl's name. "Savitri Kaapoor. Did I spell that right? Good."

"Hello Savitri," said the class. She smiled and waved back.

"OK, Savitri, you can take that seat in the back." She pointed to a seat behind Purdy. "Purdy, on lunch break would you go to the office and make copies of your notes for Savitri?"

Purdy shrugged his acceptance. As Savitri made her way to the back of the class one of the other girls put up her hand and said, "Where are you from?"

"New Jersey," said Savitri, taking her seat. She leaned forward and whispered to Purdy,

"Those notes better be good."

"Or your money back," whispered Purdy.

"All right, class," said Mrs. Martinez, "we were discussing how Revolutionary war battles were fought. The British were used to the European model of battle, which was to line the armies face to face across an open field and shoot at each other, the soldiers in the front row shooting first and then crouching down to reload while the second row shot. This model of warfare did not always work well for the American troops, and they strayed from it. Can anyone tell me the name of the South Carolina general who is said to be the father of guerrilla warfare?"

The class was silent.

"Ooh," said Joe, "we know this."

"Yes we do. Raise your hand."

"No we don't"

"Purdy," said Mrs. Martinez, "did you say something?"

"Oh, no, I mean, yes. The answer is… the answer is… what?"

"That's what I'm asking you," said Mrs. Martinez.

Joe said, "Francis Marion."

"Francis Marion," said Purdy.

"That's correct," said the teacher.

"The dude had two chick names," said a boy sitting in the center of the class.

"No comments Creighton," said the teacher. Turning back to Purdy she asked, "And do you know Francis Marion's nickname?"

"Yes we do," said Joe.

"Um, yes we do. I mean, yes I do," said Purdy.

"Just a minute, it's on the tip of my tongue," said Joe.

"Do you mind telling us?" said Mrs. Martinez. The class laughed.

"Was it 'the father of guerilla warfare'?" said Purdy.

"Besides that," said the teacher.

"Francis Marion's nickname was… was… Fran. His friends called him Fran."

"No."

"I've got it," said Joe. "The Swamp Fox."

"The Swamp Fox," said Purdy. He sat back and wiped the sweat from his forehead.

<>

Later Purdy returned from lunch break early. The classroom was empty so he had a discussion with Joe about cheating. He was against it.

"What about hints?" said Joe. "Are hints cheating?"

"Well, I guess it depends on how big a hint it is. No, I don't even want hints. I've been doing just fine without your help."

"'His friends called him Fran'? You call that doing fine? What kind of guess was that?" said Joe.

"Look, you got me into that. I didn't even want to answer that question."

The door opened and Savitri came in. "Talking to yourself again?" she said.

"Yeah, I do that." He handed her a stack of copies.

"Hey, these are good," she said, looking through the notes.

"Why did you think they wouldn't be?" said Purdy.

"Well, you know, the stupid kids usually like to sit in the back of the classroom."

"Oh, Mrs. Martinez is onto that. She puts the stupid kids right up front where she can torture them."

"I'd like to be up front," said Savitri, taking her seat and then turning and propping her feet up on the chair of the desk beside her. "I'm tired of being the class brain. I'd like to be one of the bad girls. No, not like that," she said, responding to Purdy's expression. "Maybe not bad, just dumb. You know, the kind of girl who only cares about clothes and hair and music and stuff, talking trash and snapping Z's, and never seeming to study at all."

"Good news," said Purdy. "You're sounding dumber to me by the minute."

"Really?"

"No."

"Rats," said Savitri.

"If you're really a braniac like you say, you couldn't stand not to study."

"I know," she sighed. She looked up at Purdy. "What's your name again?"

"Purdy."

"That's a dumb name," she said.

"Well, gee, thanks. That means a lot coming from you, Savitri."

Savitri sat up. "What's wrong with Savitri?" she said.

"Nothing."

"It's a nice name," she insisted.

"I was just joking," said Purdy. "You made a joke about my name so I made a joke about yours. Sorry. Jeez, you're…"

"Sensitive?" suggested Savitri.

"Yes."

"I know," she said. They sat silently for a minute. "I wasn't joking. Purdy is a dumb name. Are you named after somebody?"

"I don't know," said Purdy.

"Don't know? How can you not know about your own name?"

Purdy shrugged. "Well," he said, "are you named after someone?"

Savitri shut her eyes and let her breath escape with a long, drawn out "Uhhh." She said, "Of course I am. I'm named after Savitri."

"Oh, of course."

"She was a princess."

"Of course."

<>

After class, as Purdy was walking down the hallway he felt one of his dizzy spells coming on. He moved to the wall beside some lockers, popped a piece of chocolate in his mouth, and waited for the fog in his head to clear.

"You OK?" said Joe.

Purdy nodded. The dizzy spell passed and he continued on his way.

"There's a big blonde kid from your class coming up behind you," said Joe. "He's going to knock the books out from under your arm."

Purdy stopped and said loudly, "Creighton, it would be really lame if you knock my books down." He turned and faced the bully.

"What do you have, eyes in the back of your head?" said Creighton.

"Yes," said Purdy, turning away.

"Oh yeah, Hooper, then tell me how many fingers I'm holding up?"

"One," said Joe.

"One," said Purdy.

"Wait," said Creighton. "Lucky guess. Let me try again."

"Five," said Purdy. "Now three, two, seven. One again."

"You must have a mirror or something," said Creighton. As Purdy started to leave the bully grabbed his shoulder and said, "No, wait, one more time. How many fingers?"

"He's lifting his foot to kick you in the butt," said Joe.

Purdy turned quickly and grabbed the foot. "Eyes in the back of my head," he said. "Don't mess with me anymore." He lifted the foot higher. Creighton began hopping backwards to keep his balance and fell into a group of girls.

"Four-eyed geek," Creighton called after him.

"Thanks Joe," Purdy whispered as he walked away.

"No trouble. Just gave you a few hints."

In the evening Doreen's tongue stuck out the side of her mouth as she concentrated on painting a face on a small inverted clay flowerpot. She was seated at the newspaper covered kitchen table, making angel wind chimes, which she would try to sell later in the year at church bazaars to raise money for Christmas presents. Flower pots, being very brittle, are not the ideal material for wind chimes or angels, so there were broken angels hanging all around their home, inside and out. Purdy watched her and waited for her to put down her brush.

"Mom, was I named after Dad?"

"Now don't be silly. You know your Dad's named Ronald."

"What was his middle name?"

"What is his middle name?" she corrected.

"What is his middle name?" asked Purdy.

"Don't you know? Ronald Clark Hooper."

Purdy thought a moment. "Was I named after an uncle, or grandfather, or someone?"

Doreen dunked her paintbrush in a coffee cup half filled with grey water. "Sillier and sillier," she said. "Haven't I told you the story of how you got your name? I'm sure I must have. Listen, come sit on the couch. I'll tell you all about it."

They moved to the couch and Doreen sat cross-legged at one end, her hands pressed together in front of her face as she collected her thoughts. When she was ready she opened her hands wide and began speaking. "Before you were born your Daddy and I picked out some nice names, beautiful names. Both boy and girl names – even with ultrasound pictures you can never be too sure. I was partial to Arliss."

"Arliss?"

"Oh, hush, it's nice. I had an uncle Arliss. Such a nice man 'till he got run over by his own truck, twice, which is a whole other story. Back to names. Your Daddy was voting for Gregory. Anyway, when you come to be born, I was in labor for…"

"Eighteen hours," said Purdy. "You tell me every time you're mad at me."

"That's right, I was in labor for eighteen hours. You have no idea. Pushing out a big head like yours ain't no walk in the park."

"Mama!"

"Well, it's true. It was really hard on me, and near the end I was pretty much out of it, what with the pain, and drugs, and, well, eighteen hours. I was beater than beat. So I look up and there's this nurse holding a baby and she says, 'What's his name?' So I'm thinking, 'How on Earth should I know your baby's name?' But she keeps standing there, so I'm looking at this baby, and it's about the ugliest baby I ever saw – all red and squished up and wet. My Mama always taught me to be polite, though, so I said, 'he's purdy.'

"Later when I woke up I saw you sleeping in the little plastic crib next to my bed, and on the name tag above your head the nurse had written, 'Purdy Hooper.' I liked it, so when it came time to fill out the birth certificate that's the name we put down."

Purdy jumped up off the couch. "Wait a minute," he said. "Back up, back up, time out." He struggled to find the words. "Are you trying to… my name… you're telling me my name is 'Pretty?'"

Doreen shook her head.

"Oh my gosh, oh my gosh! What kind of name is that for a boy? I don't believe this." He felt his face turning red and put his hands over it, then threw them down. "You gosh darn hillbilly!" he shouted, and stomped out of the room.

5

On **Sunday afternoon,** Purdy rode his bicycle to the Stop 'N' Shop to refill his "medicine" prescription. Once inside he was surprised to find Savitri sitting behind the counter beside the cigarettes and dirty magazines, watching a small TV set. "Hey, Savitri," he said.

"Hey, Purdy."

"I didn't know you had a job."

"It's not a job, really," she said. "I'm just helping out my family."

"Oh? Oh, I see. Amar is your dad. Now, why didn't I figure that out?"

"Well, duh!" said Savitri. "How many Indians do you know in this little town?"

"A lot," said Purdy.

"You know what I mean. India Indians, not Native Americans."

"Just hadn't thought about it, I guess. Well, this is cool. I bet you get to have any candy and stuff you want free."

Savitri gave him a hard look. "You're not getting anything free from me," she said.

"Oh, no, that's not what I meant," said Purdy. "You know, I like your dad – he's nice. You must be adopted."

"Ha, ha."

"I'll be right back," said Purdy, and he went to the back of the store to agonize over which candy to purchase. He settled on a "Super Sour Mouth Buster" which, according to the commercials, was guaranteed to detach your head from your body and send it rocketing into space. He counted out his change before he got back to the front counter, so as not to give Savitri an opportunity to remind him that he had to pay for his candy.

"Here you go," he said, waving his candy in front of the scanner and pushing the change toward Savitri. "So, how do you like Desert Tortoise Elementary School so far?"

"I've been in better," said Savitri, as she separated the change into the correct compartments in the cash register drawer, "but I've been in worse too. We've moved around a lot. It's not too bad." She slammed the drawer shut and leaned across the counter. "So, tell me all the dirt," she said.

"What?"

"You know, the inside story. The gossip. Who's cheating, who's smoking, who's hot for who?"

"Look," said Purdy, "I haven't been in our class much longer than you have."

""But you've been in our school longer. You must know these kids."

"I've only been here four years. My mom and I moved down from Phoenix."

"Well, for example, what's the deal with… what's his name? Creighton?" Savitri asked, looking down and playing with the beads on her necklace.

"Oh, Satan Creighton. Just picks on littler guys. Thinks he's cool. Why, has he bothered you?"

"Oh, no, no. He's a neighbor, that's all."

"Yeah, well, just stay out of his way and you'll be alright."

<>

Outside again after making his purchase Purdy was climbing onto his bicycle when Joe said, "She's cute."

"How old are you?" Purdy said. "Perv."

"No, no," said Joe. "I meant she's cute for you."

"Yeah, well no thanks. I'm too young."

"Too young to like girls?"

"No," said Purdy. "Not exactly. Just too young to admit it."

"Oh, yes, I remember how that was. Still, I think she likes you."

"You're nuts," said Purdy. He turned onto a dirt road that was a shortcut home. The road passed through an open stretch of desert. Casi Nada is located in the northern half of the Sonoran Desert. The Sonoran is not the stereotypical desert most people picture in their minds – no sand dunes or camels. The ground is covered with rocks, and, thanks to two brief rainy seasons each year, it is, by desert standards, a garden. You cannot go two feet in any direction without encountering vegetation of some sort – cactus, small shrubs, or desert trees, and there is that space, as if the plants were carefully laid out by a landscaper with a yardstick. One can imagine the roots of the plants slugging it out underground to reserve their small portion of water. In its prickly territorial possessiveness, the desert is the most human of landscapes. Wildlife is plentiful too. Rabbits, lizards, and birds scamper about as if auditioning for an old Disney cartoon, but most of the animals only come out at night.

Purdy had to ride his bicycle more slowly on the bumpy parts of the dirt road, and as he slowed a thought occurred to him. "Am I going too fast for you?" he said. "Are you, like, running alongside me?"

"Oh, no, not running. More like flying or floating," said Joe, "and you aren't going too fast. I can go as fast as I want – faster than cars, faster than planes if I want to."

"Wow, that's pretty cool."

"I suppose. Right now I'm floating just ahead of you, travelling backwards so I can see you when you speak. I can't get too far away because my

thoughts seem to carry about as far as real speech would. That is, you seem to be able to hear me only as far away as you would if I were actually talking."
Purdy thought about this for a moment. "So, aren't you talking? Does your mouth move when you say something?"

"Yes, I talk when I talk to you, my mouth moves, and I can hear it in here, though maybe I'm only hearing my voice in my head like you do. I don't think I'm making real sound that your world can hear. The air doesn't touch me here. There's no wind in my face when I travel fast. Without air I don't think I can really make sound. The human voice is a wind instrument. You force air up into your throat and vibrate your vocal cords to make sound. I can hear your world perfectly well, though I don't know how. I wish I had learned more about science. I'm pretty sure no oxygen means no sound. There's sound under water, though. I just don't know."

Purdy stopped riding so he could experiment. He closed his mouth, held his nose, and made a humming sound. "See?" he said, "Sound with no air."
"You're still forcing air up into your throat even though you aren't letting it out. Close your mouth, hold your nose, and try to make sound while you try to inhale."

Silence.
"See?" said Joe.
"I guess." Purdy rode on and said, "Do you want to play 'Dude?'"
"Sure, how do you play?"
"You just say 'Dude.'"
"You just say 'Dude?'" Joe repeated.
"Yep."
"OK, you start."
"Dude," said Purdy.
"Dude."
"Dude"
"Dude."
"Yo, Dude," said Purdy.
"'Yo yo Dude."
"Don't have a yo-yo, Dude."
"Bummer, Dude," said Joe.
"Totally, Dude."
"Cockadoodle Dude."
"OK, that's enough," said Purdy, laughing.
"Listen, Dude," said Joe. "I have something serious to discuss with you. We have a problem."

Purdy stopped and put his hand up. "Whoa," he said. "We do not have problems. There is no we. Your voice may be inside my head but that hardly make us Siamese Twins, or something. So, you can have a problem, I can have a problem. We do not have problems."

"Are you finished?"

"Oui."

"Good. We have a problem," said Joe. "It's about your mom."

"My mom?" Purdy got off his bicycle. "What about my mom?"

"A guy at her job at the supermarket has been harassing her. You know, hitting on her."

The bicycle fell over, raising a cloud of dust. "Someone's hitting my mom?"

"No, Purdy, no. Not hitting her, hitting on her. It means, like, asking her out."

"Is that all?" Purdy slapped his hands on his pants in disgust. "Dude, you scared me. And why were you watching my mom at the supermarket anyway?"

"I, uh… you're important to me. I need you. So, naturally, if I'm concerned about you, I'm concerned about your family."

Purdy spun the wheel of his bicycle with his foot. "Selfish and thoughtful. Nice combination there, Joe. Sometimes I'm not sure if you're a nice guy or not."

"Of course, you're right," Joe said. "You can't trust strangers. I am a nice guy but I can't convince you by anything I say. I'll have to earn your trust. I'm trying to do that. That's why I'm telling you I think your mom needs our help."

"Are we back to that?" Purdy said. He put his hands in his pockets and started pacing back and forth. "What's the big deal if someone asked her out?"

"She's married, for one thing."

"Yeah, but my dad left seven or eight years ago. He's probably dead."

"You think so?"

"I wish I knew," said Purdy, scowling. "I guess it doesn't matter one way or the other, but it would be easier if I knew for sure."

"And you mom? What does she think?"

Purdy thought back to the last time he had made the mistake of asking his mom that question. Though she cried easily, cried watching greeting card commercials, she didn't often let him see her get really upset, so it always alarmed him a little when she did. As soon as he said, "Do you think Dad is dead?" Doreen's eyes filled with tears, just as suddenly as if a switch had been flipped. "I don't know," she stammered. "I mean, I don't think so. I mean…" She tapped her hand on her heart. "I would know it. Don't you think? Don't you think I would have to know it? How could I not? He's alive. I would know." Purdy had watched her turn away and never asked again.

"She thinks he's alive. Totally," said Purdy.

"See, there?" said Joe. "So of course she wouldn't want to be asked out, but it's worse than that. Let me tell you what I saw so you can judge for yourself.

This morning, at the supermarket, your mom was at her check-stand as usual. When she got a break she went into the employee's lounge. There were two men in there; an old man with pants up to his armpits…"

"That's Gordy," said Purdy. "He's just a bagger."

"Yes, and another young guy, tall, black hair."

"Uh, that's probably Rick. He's also a checker, like my mom."

"Yes. Well, when your mom came in, Rick said, 'Hey Sugar, how about some sugar?' and your mom said, 'Sugar is on aisle seven.' He crowded her up against the lockers and said, 'How come you won't go out with me? I've asked a hundred times. We'd have a good time.' Your mom said, 'No, thank you.' Then he grabbed her wrist. 'Let go, please,' your mom said, and he said he wouldn't until she agreed to go out with him. She put her hand over his and began to squeeze his thumb. 'Ouch, ouch, ouch!' he said, and let go right away but she kept hold and he said, 'Ouch, ouch, ouch,' until he was on his knees on the floor."

"Go, Mom!" said Purdy.

"Your mom said, 'Oh, I'm sorry, did that hurt? Aspirin is on aisle eleven.' and she turned and left. The old guy snickered, and Rick said, 'Shut up!' He got up and kicked the lockers. 'Next time she'll be the one on her knees,' he said."

"What a jerk," said Purdy. "Maybe my mom will complain to the boss."

"She's too stubborn. Thinks she can handle anything," said Joe.

"I guess you're right. So what do we do?"

"We have to get rid of him."

Purdy stopped his pacing. "You don't mean kill him? He's just a jerk. He hasn't really done anything yet."

"You watch too much TV. No, not kill him. Just get rid of him. Get him out of this town."

"How am I supposed to do that?"

"I'll watch him for a while," said Joe. "He's hardly a sterling character. I'm sure he has some secret we can use against him."

"What if he doesn't have any secrets?" said Purdy.

"Everyone has secrets."

<>

6

That evening at dinner, Purdy asked, as innocently as he could, "Mom, does anyone ever bother you at work?"

Doreen put down her slice of pizza. "Where are you hurt?" she said.

"What? I'm not hurt."

"If there's someone bothering you I want to know. I'll stomp them into the ground."

"No one's bothering me," said Purdy. "I was talking about you. You know how there are bullies at school? I was just wondering if there were bullies at work too."

Doreen relaxed back in her chair. "Oh, no. Not really."

"No one ever bothers you?"

"Oh, well, I guess they would if I let them. When I was a kid our family was pretty poor, but we lived in a small town where most everyone was kin, and we were all pretty poor so we kids didn't even know we were poor. When I got to high school, though, I had to take a bus to the next town over where some of the kids weren't as poor as we were. Sometimes the girls at school would make fun of my raggedy old hand-me-down clothes. One day I came home crying about that, and my Granny, Rose Eller, took me aside and said, 'Baby, I got a secret to tell you.' and she took me 'round to the back of the house and she whispered in my ear, 'Everyone else is nuts.' Well, that opened my eyes. Suddenly the world was so much easier to understand. And you can't really stay mad at someone very long if you know they're nuts because, well, they don't know no better. So those girls at school could just laugh themselves sick and it didn't bother me no more because I knew my clothes were beautiful, and I was beautiful, and if they couldn't see that, well, they were just nuts. So you remember what my Granny told me, Darlin'. I think it will be a help to you."

"I will, Mama."

<>

The next day in the school cafeteria Purdy was carrying his tray, looking for a place to sit when he saw Savitri placing her tray down at an empty table. He set his tray down across from hers. "Saving this place for anybody?" he said.

"Nope. Free country. Sit down."

"My hot dog won't bother you?"

"Excuse me?" said Savitri.

"I figure you're a vegetarian and all."

"Oh. No. Sit down."

He sat down and tore open a packet of mustard for his hot dog and a packet of ketchup for his fries. "You know," he said, "Mrs. Martinez is going to pair us off to do those reports on the signers of the Declaration of Independence. I was wondering if you wanted to pair up with me?"

Savitri looked up at him, then looked around the room. "Well, I…"

"Of course, if you already have someone else, or you'd rather work with a girl…"

"No, no."

"I'd rather work alone," said Purdy. "Whenever I'm on a team I end up doing all the work myself anyway."

"Yeah, me too," said Savitri. "O.K., I'll work with you."

"OK," said Purdy. He reached to open his bottle of cola, and cried, "Aaaaah!" as the soda rushed up. By the time he got the cap back on, his hot dog and fries were afloat.

"Don't you even know how to open a bottle of soda?" said Savitri sternly. "How old are you? You should know better by now. Watch me, I'll show you how it's done." She reached for her bottle. "You twist it ever so slightly, listen for the gas escaping, let it out slowly, slowly. When you don't hear it anymore then you open it all the way. See?"

Purdy watched the entire demonstration without expression. When it was over he reached across the table and gave her plastic bottle a quick squeeze, sending a geyser of soda into the air. "Delayed reaction," he said.

"Purdy!" yelled Savitri angrily, but when she saw him laughing she couldn't help but laugh herself. They dumped their soggy trays into the nearest trash can, and Purdy went to the restroom to wash his hands.

Back in class, as Purdy predicted, Mrs. Martinez announced, "I'd like you to find a partner, and we'll head on over to the library to research our reports on the signers of the Declaration of Independence. Once you decide who you'd like to report on, see me. I'll have a sign-up sheet. I don't want fifteen reports on Benjamin Franklin."

The class erupted into motion as students raced up and down the aisles to find partners. Purdy, having already found a partner, calmly arranged his notebook, and tucked a couple of pencils into his pocket. When he finally turned back toward Savitri, he found her speaking to Creighton.

"So you want to work together?" said Creighton.

"Um, sure," said Savitri. They both looked at Purdy.

"What you looking at, Hooper?" said Creighton.

"Nothing," said Purdy, turning away.

"Go on ahead," said Savitri to Creighton. "I'll meet you in the library."

Creighton headed up the aisle, barely pausing to knock Purdy's notebook onto the floor. As Purdy bent to pick up his notebook, Savitri said, "I'm sorry. I forgot you already asked me."

"It's OK, I don't care," said Purdy. "Go."

Savitri left the room. Instead of looking around for another partner, Purdy sat back and waited, hoping there were an odd number of students in class that day so he would be left without a partner. He was in luck. "No partner, Purdy?" said Mrs. Martinez. "Let's see, Dennis is out sick today. You can work with him when he returns. OK?"

"Sure," said Purdy, hoping, though not in a bad way, that Dennis would remain sick until the project was over. As he walked to the library he tried to make sense out of what Savitri had done. He couldn't believe she didn't remember she had agreed to work with him. It wasn't so long ago. There were spots on his shirt that were still damp from the exploding cola. If she did remember, she had lied, but why? He didn't care if she wanted to work with Creighton, though why anyone would want to work with Creighton was an entirely separate mystery. Had she been afraid to say no to him? Maybe she didn't want to work with Creighton at all. Purdy realized he could have saved her from that by speaking up, by saying, "She's working with me." Perhaps if he hadn't taken so much time arranging his notebook they'd have left for the library before Creighton even made it to her desk. He recognized, before this line of argument got too far advanced that it was just one of his hero fantasies. "Maybe Savitri doesn't want to work with me," he thought, "and had lied in the cafeteria." That seemed much more likely, but, again, why lie? To Purdy, things had to make sense – if they didn't it was only because they hadn't been figured out yet. He was finding, however, that the path of logic seldom leads all the way to the end of a woman's thoughts. This was irritating, and more irritating still – intriguing. He paused for a dizzy spell and a chocolate before entering the library.

When Purdy got home from school, Joe was waiting for him. "Hello, Purdy. Good day at school?"

"No lousier than usual," said Purdy. "Hold on." He took out his cell phone and dialed.

"Every day I have to call my mom to let her know I got home OK," he explained. He let the phone ring a few times and hung up. "She sees it's me."

"Well, good news," said Joe. "We've got him."

"Got who?" Purdy tossed his backpack under his desk and kicked off his shoes.

"What do you mean, 'who?' Who have I been following around? Rick, the guy who's bothering your mom."

"Oh, yeah. So, how have we got him?"

"I heard him on the phone last night, arranging to sell some drugs to a friend in a couple of days."

"OK," Purdy said slowly, "but how does that help us?"

"Simple," said Joe. "You make an anonymous call to the police, they arrest him, and he's out of the way for a while. Maybe for good."

"Heck no," said Purdy. "I can't do that."

"Why not?"

"Well, what if he's just selling aspirin or something?"

"You know it's not aspirin."

"Yeah, OK, but you said he's just selling some stuff to his friend. It's not like he's some big time drug dealer."

"What's the problem here, Purdy?"

Purdy flopped onto his bed and stared at the ceiling for a while. "The problem is I can't send him to jail. I watch TV. Bad things happen in jail. I can't be responsible for that."

"You're not responsible," said Joe. "He's the one who chose to do something illegal. He's the one treating your mother badly. He's responsible, not you."

"Still," said Purdy. He sat up. "I've got a better idea. Did you see where he has the drugs hidden?"

"Yes. He keeps some in his mattress and some in a hole in the floor under the carpet in his closet."

"Good." Purdy hopped off the bed and turned on his computer, which sat on a milk crate in the corner. Once it had warmed up he began typing. "Dear Rick," he began, then went back and deleted "Dear."

"Rick,

You don't know me. I shouldnt help you cause I think you're trash, but I like the cops even less. The cops are onto you. They know you got drugs hiddin in you bed and in that hole in your closet. They knows about the deal with your friend in a couple of days, and are waiting to arrest both of you. Your only chance to stay out of jail is to get out of the state in 24 hours and stay out. I don't think you is smart enough to listen, but you should."

Purdy read over the letter, went back and threw in a few more spelling errors, then hit the print button. "OK," he said, "now just tell me where he lives and I'll slip this letter under his door."

"You're right," said Joe, "that was a better idea. I was worried he'd get off with a warning. This will get him out of the state altogether. You're a genius."

"Yeah, yeah," said Purdy, putting his shoes back on. "Let's get this over with."

<>

The next afternoon Purdy's cell phone rang. "Hello, Darlin'," said Doreen. "I'm going to be late getting home. One of our checkers didn't show up for work today, so we're extra busy."

Purdy smiled.

<>

7

Purdy never knew when Joe would pop into his head. Sometimes that now-familiar voice would pipe up with comments every few minutes, other times it would be gone for days at a time. "Hello, Purdy," said Joe one afternoon after a few days absence. Purdy was sitting on a lawn-chair in the small fenced-in yard behind the mobile home. He was hunched over, intently scraping the bottom of one of his sneakers with a sharpened Popsicle stick.

"What is it with dogs?" Purdy burst out. "Do they think the whole world is their toilet? Dogs are smarter than cats, aren't they?" He didn't wait for an answer. "They're way smarter. You can't tell me a dog can't learn to poop in a box the way cats do. If I had a dog the first thing I'd do is get a big ol' litter box and say, 'Look, pee wherever the heck you want to, but you have to poop in the box.' And what's the deal with sneakers? Why do they always have to have all these little tiny grooves on the bottom? I'll tell you why. It's so when you step in dog poop it's impossible to clean and you have to throw the stupid thing out and buy a new pair. Aaargh!" He tossed down the stick, turned, and threw his sneaker. The sneaker neatly clipped the head off of one of his mother's beloved pink plastic flamingos that stood in a row at the border of her small, carefully tended garden.

"Oh man," said Purdy. He got up and picked up the flamingo head. "Oh man! I'll be right back. I've got to get some super glue." After a couple of minutes he returned with the glue and set about repairing the flamingo. "I'm sorry," he said. "I get mad about the stupidest stuff."

"No need to apologize," said Joe. "You can't help how you feel. You just have to be careful not to let your feelings boss you."

"What?"

"My dad used to say, 'Control your emotions – float. Your emotions control you – sink.'"

"Huh," said Purdy, gingerly releasing his hold on the lawn ornament's neck and stepping back to inspect his work. "So, your dad wrote fortune cookies?"

"Listen, wise guy, I'm just trying to be helpful."

"I know, I know."

"Along those lines, I guess I have some more bad news," said Joe.

Purdy sat down heavily in the lawn-chair. "Oh jeez, you're getting to be such a ray of sunshine, you know that Joe?"

"I know."

"Well, what is it this time? Someone beating on my mom again?"

"No, this time it's about you."

"Well?" asked Purdy."

"I think somebody is going to try to kidnap you."

Purdy snickered. "Yeah, right. Who would want to kidnap me?"

"I don't know."

"So why would you think someone would try to kidnap me?"

After a pause Joe replied, "I've seen it."

"You've seen it? What, like you've seen the future?" Purdy stood up and began to pace. Pacing always helped him think. "Look, you've told me all kinds of goofy things, like you can fly, and go through walls, and all that, and I've believed it, pretty much. Now you're trying to tell me you can see the future? I'm sorry, that is just too much."

"It's not like that, exactly," said Joe. "I had a dream."

"You had a dream. Jeez. So, wait a minute, you mean you sleep in Sockworld?"

"Yes, of course. Why would you think I wouldn't?"

"Well, you don't do anything else, don't breathe or eat."

"I do get tired," said Joe. "Mentally tired, so, yes, I do sleep. I sleep quite a bit."

"So how does that work? I mean, if there's no gravity there aren't you afraid that when you're sleeping you'll go floating off into space?"

"I was afraid at first, but it's an interesting thing. When you're not trying to go anywher then slowly you just sink back to the ground, or if you go underground then you float up to the surface."

"You can go underground?"

"Well, by accident sometimes. Not something you'd want to do. It's dark. So, anyway, it doesn't seem like it's gravity that draws you to the ground. It's more like, hmmm, like a sense of belonging that brings you back."

"OK, so you were sleeping and had a bad dream," said Purdy. "So what?"

"In Sockworld, sometimes dreams come true."

"Dreams come true. Aww, isn't that sweet?" Purdy tired of walking back and forth wearing only one sneaker, so he retrieved the stick he had been using, picked up the sneaker he had thrown, and went back to work scraping the dog poop off the bottom.

"It's not sweet," Joe insisted. "It's awful. Imagine dreaming something bad is going to happen, and then later you see it really happen. It's a curse, really… knowing. It's like you see an accident is about to take place and you know nothing can stop it. It's like having to experience a bad thing twice. Do you remember that house fire in town about a month ago?"

"Down by the railroad tracks?"

"Yes. Well, about two weeks before the fire I dreamed that I saw that house burning."

"It's called a coincidence," said Purdy. You have a dream and it doesn't come true, then it's just a dream. You have a dream and it does come true and suddenly, 'Ooh, I can tell the future.'

No, it's just coincidence."

"I wish I could believe that, but it's happened to me too many times to be coincidence."

"But it, it… it has to be," Purdy said emphatically. "What else could it be? You can't see the future. The future hasn't even happened so there is nothing to see."

"I know, but what if time doesn't work the way we think it does? People invented time. Maybe we got it wrong."

"Wrong how?"

"OK," said Joe, "let's picture the way we think of time as a road made of bricks. The brick you are standing on is the present. There are no bricks ahead of you yet. The road ends right at your feet. Now you know that there is a road in back of you, the past, because you were just there a second ago, but you can't turn around and look at it. You're only equipped to see the present. Of course you know the past is right behind you. You see evidence of it everywhere, but you can only see the moment you're in. You can't turn back and see the moment before, much less see George Washington, or dinosaurs walking around. You take a step forward, a new brick appears under your feet, and you can no longer see the brick you were just standing on. So, time is a road that is building itself, moment by moment, brick by brick."

"Right," said Purdy.

"OK. Now suppose we use a different picture of time. In this picture the entire road is built; past, present, and future. You can still only see the brick you're standing on at the time. The road ahead is there already – you just can't see it, the same way you can't see the road in back of you. You're still only equipped to see the present, but all time exists all at once. The world would still look exactly the same to you, even if the future already exists. But maybe this road isn't straight. Maybe it's like a mountain road that curves all around. Maybe sometimes, just for a moment, you get a glimpse off to your side of the road ahead, a little sneak peek of the future?"

Purdy put down his sneaker again and thought hard about this new concept. Finally, he shook his head. "It can't be that way. If the future exists, if everything that's going to happen is already there, it's like it already happened, and if it already happened it's not the future, it's the past. Time can't all be the past. If everything is already planned out, then what? Are we all just walking along reading some script that has already been written? What would be the point?"

"What is the point now?" asked Joe.

"The point now? The point now is… the point now is… aaah!" Purdy screamed when he realized that he had been tapping his chin with the stick he had been using to scrape dog poop. "Stupid nonsense! Look what you made me do. How the heck should I know what the point is? No, wait, I do. I'll tell you what the point is. The point is — if the future doesn't already exist, then what we do matters. That's the point."

Joe said, "You have a point. I'm just not sure mattering matters."

"What?"

"I mean, well, do you think a chicken experiences time?"

"Yes, I guess," said Purdy. "I mean yeah, it must. 'Time to lay that egg. Time to eat that bug. Time to cross the road.'"

"And do you think a chicken spends much of its time worrying if what it does matters? Of course things happen because of what we do. Even if the future is already out there we go on making our decisions and causing the things that will occur to occur."

Purdy pressed his hands over his eyes. He liked to watch the constantly changing kaleidoscope of colors and shapes that shifted and bloomed on the movie screen of his eyelids. "No," he said wearily. "The future is not already there. Sorry, no. No, no, no. It just wouldn't make sense. You'll just have to figure out some other reason your dreams come true."

Joe said, "I do have another theory. Maybe in Sockworld you just get a better sense of consequences. Nothing just happens. Everything happens because something before it happened, and something before that. Like dominoes set up in a row. You just don't get a sunburn on top of your head. First you look in a magazine and see a picture of a guy with a bald head. You think, 'Oh, that would be a good look for me.' You get out your scissors. You cut off your hair. You shave your head. You go outside to mow the lawn. You get a sunburn on the top of your head. Nothing just happens. Maybe in Sockworld you have a clearer view of the way those dominoes are going to fall."

Purdy conceded that the second theory, if still goofy, seemed much more likely than that the future existed. "So tell me about this scary dream," he said.

"Someone was grabbing you. Trying to take you to his truck."

"Who?"

"I don't know," said Joe. "You don't always see things clearly in dreams. I never saw him before. All I remember is that he had tattoos."

"Oh, gee, that narrows it down," said Purdy. "I know kids whose grandmas have tattoos.

Everyone has tattoos now. It's like everyone in the world is a flippin' sailor. Well, I'm not going to worry about it."

"I wish you would," said Joe. "I've seen it happen. It's going to happen. You must be careful."

"Yeah, yeah, I will," Purdy assured him, but thought to himself that the whole thing was just a stupid, meaningless dream. He put on his sneaker, rubbed it in the gravel, then went inside to wash his chin and have a snack.

The flamingo's head fell to the ground.

<>

8

"I know which girl in class you like best," whispered Savitri.

Purdy looked around. "Why are you whispering," he asked. "The classroom is empty."

Savitri shrugged and repeated, "I know which girl you like best."

"Not you," said Purdy.

"Not me."

Purdy thought a few moments. "I give up," he said. "Which one?"

"Tammy."

"Tammy? Why Tammy?"

"Duh," said Savitri. "Isn't it obvious? I see the way all you boys stare at her. It's because she has the biggest chi-chi's so far."

"Aaah!" shouted Purdy. "You can't say that."

"What, chi-chi's?"

"Aaah! You said it again."

"Well, that's what all the girls here call them. What do you want me to call them? B…"

Purdy clapped his hand over her mouth. "I don't want you to call them anything. We cannot be talking about this. Now, I'm going to take my hand away and you are not going to say anything. OK?"

Savitri nodded, and Purdy slowly removed his hand. Savitri was silent. Purdy sighed in relief and sat back in his chair.

"Boobies," said Savitri.

"Aaah!" shouted Purdy, getting up. "That's it. I'm out of here."

"Oh, sit down," said Savitri. "What's the big deal?"

"Look," said Purdy, "this is not something boys and girls discuss, especially not in school. You talk to me sometimes like I'm one of your girlfriends."

"Well, you're not my boyfriend, are you?"

"Heck no."

"So if you're not my boyfriend, and you're not my girlfriend, how am I supposed to talk to you?" asked Savitri. "Like you're my dog? Sit boy. Stay."

Purdy wavered a moment, then sat down. They were both quiet for a minute. "The whole thing is stupid," Purdy said. "I'm supposed to like Tammy best just because she has the biggest you-know-whats? It's stupid. She doesn't anyway. Olivia's are just as big."

"Those aren't real," said Savitri.

"What? What do you mean? No, never mind. I don't want to know."

"So you like Olivia, huh?"

"I didn't say that."

"I'm not worried," said Savitri. "My mom has big ones, so I will too."

Purdy's forehead slammed onto his desktop with a loud thud. "Oh, God, please tell me we are not discussing your mom's… your mom's…"

"My mom's what?"

Purdy slammed his forehead down again. "Please, make it stop."

Several students filed in the open door. Purdy sat up, rubbing his forehead. He turned and whispered, "I know which boy you like best."

"I don't like you," said Savitri.

"I know."

<>

After school, Purdy rode his bicycle to the Stop 'N' Shop to replenish his candy supply. In the past few weeks his dizzy spells had been coming more frequently, so he found himself buying candy almost every other day. Candy bars didn't last long enough, so he had been choosing candy that came in small pieces, like M&M'S, or Skittles, and popping them like pills.

"Howdy," he said as he entered the store.

"Hey, how you doin'?" said Amar, from behind the counter. Purdy headed down the candy aisle. As he was studying the selection, the bell on the door jingled and two young men in long coats came in. One came toward Purdy, and as he turned to get past him in the narrow aisle, Purdy saw the handle of a gun poking out of his pants. Purdy looked up and briefly glimpsed a black and red tattoo of a rattlesnake on the man's neck. The man went on past him toward the back of the store. Purdy dropped the package of candy he had been holding. He knew somehow that the two men were going to rob the place. His heart was beating hard. He felt it beating in his throat, which had never happened to him. He thought he might be having a heart attack. "Great," he thought, "I'm going to drop dead and then get shot." After several moments of not dropping dead he determined it was not a heart attack. "Joe," he whispered, "are you here?" No reply. "What good are you?"

He wanted to run very badly, but found he could barely move. He made his way slowly up the aisle. He knew he had to warn Amar somehow, but one of the men was at the front of the store looking at magazines, or at least pretending to. He could see both men were watching him, waiting for him to leave.

As Purdy approached the cash register Amar looked up and said, "Hey, how about an apple today?" He picked up an apple from the basket on the counter. "It's very good."

"Um, no thanks," said Purdy. "I think I'll just take some chips." He grabbed a large bag of potato chips from a rack and ran out the door.

"Hey!" shouted Amar. "Hey!" He ran around the counter and out after the boy. He found Purdy standing in the parking lot, and grabbed him by the collar. "What you think you're doing?" he said angrily.

Purdy shifted so Amar was blocking his view of the store, and said, "Those men have guns. I think they're going to rob you."

Amar loosened his grip. "Oh my goodness."

"No," said Purdy, "don't look around. They're probably watching us."

"Oh my goodness. What will we do?"

"Here," said Purdy, "Take these and give me that." He handed Amar the bag of chips and his cell phone, and took the apple from his hand. "Call the police, but first push me on the ground."

"What?"

"You have to make it look like you're calling the police about me."

"Oh," said Amar. "Very good." He shouted, "Thief! Scoundrel!" and gave Purdy a gentle push. Purdy rolled his eyes and fell to the ground. As Amar dialed, Purdy crawled behind the one car in the parking lot.

"Yes, emergency," Amar whispered into the phone. "Thieves in my store. Two. No, I'm outside. Amar Kaapoor. It's the Stop 'N' Shop on the corner of Saguaro and Third. Saguaro! I don't care how you pronounce it."

"Tell them they're driving a white Toyota with red doors," said Purdy, emerging from behind the car.

"They're not driving," said Amar.

"They're not going to wait for the police," said Purdy.

Amar grinned. "You're so clever. Yes," he said into the phone, "they're driving a white Toyota with red doors. Yes, hurry."

Amar handed the phone back to Purdy. "Now what?" he said.

Purdy said, "Chase me," grabbed the bag of chips out of Amar's hand, and ran around the corner of the building.

"Come back!" shouted Amar. "Thief! Miscreant!"

Crouching by the side of the store Purdy and Amar heard car doors slam and the car screech out of the parking lot. Once in the street, however, it began to sputter and lurch, moving very slowly.

"Ha," said Amar, "their car don't go so good."

"Your car wouldn't go too good either with an apple stuffed in the tail-pipe," said Purdy. They watched the car crawling forward, then there was a loud pop as the apple shot out of the tailpipe and the car jumped ahead, only to screech to a stop again as a sheriff's car turned in front of it. Another Sheriff's car turned the corner and came up behind them. Soon the two young men from the store emerged from the car with their hands in the air.

Purdy knew news travelled fast in small towns, so he called his mom before she could hear about the incident from someone else. She arrived in her old blue Chevy in minutes.

"I don't understand," she said to one of the deputies. "We moved from

Phoenix to get away from crime. I thought this was a nice, quiet little town."

"Yes, ma'am," said the deputy. "Just a nice quiet little town by the side of the illegal drug superhighway out of Mexico."

"Oops," said Doreen.

"Yes, ma'am," said the deputy. "Oops."

<>

Later, when Purdy was alone in his bedroom, Joe stopped by to congratulate him. "I heard all about it," said Joe. "You helped capture two men who were wanted in a string of robberies. You were very brave."

"I wish people would stop saying that," said Purdy. "I wasn't brave. I was scared stiff."

"Of course. You can't be brave without being scared. Being brave means you're scared but you go ahead and do what you need to do anyway. So, tell me, how did you know they were going to rob the place?"

"Well, I…" Purdy swiveled his chair back and forth. How had he known? It had all seemed so clear at the time, but now, looking back, he wasn't so sure. "I saw one guy's gun."

"OK, but this is gun-happy Arizona. You've seen guys with guns before. What else was there? Did they say something? Do something?"

Purdy replayed the scene in his mind. "No, I just knew. You know how sometimes you just know something? They seemed familiar. Maybe I'd seen them on the news or something."

"Maybe. Hmm, interesting."

"Anyway, you were wrong."

"Wrong about what?" asked Joe.

"You said a guy with a tattoo would try to kidnap me. There was a guy with a tattoo but he never tried to kidnap me. The future didn't turn out the way you said. You were wrong."

"Yes, I guess so. Well, I've never been happier to be wrong about something."

They heard a knock at the front door, and Purdy got up to answer it, but when he opened his bedroom door he saw his mom had beaten him to it.

"Won't you come in, dear?" said Doreen. "OK, just a moment." She turned, then seeing Purdy said, "It's for you."

"For me?" said Purdy. "Not another reporter." When he got to the door he saw Savitri standing at the bottom of the stairs holding a large gift basket. He could see through the plastic wrapping that the basket was filled with candy, and a few pieces of fruit. At the curb of the yard he could see Amar sitting in the driver's seat of his station wagon. Purdy smiled and waved. "Hey, Savitri," he said.

"Hey, Purdy."

"Is that for me?"

"Like, duh, yeah," said Savitri.

"Wow!" Purdy came down the steps and reached out to take the basket. As he did, Savitri put her hand around his neck and pulled him forward. Pressing her lips against his ear she whispered, "Thank you." She released him and quickly turned away before he could see the tears on her cheeks. As she walked away she said, "I still don't like you."

"I know," said Purdy, touching his ear.

9

Purdy heard the first bell ring and walked quickly down the school's main hallway when a boy he didn't know said to him, "Hey, gotta pee?" Another boy turned and said, "Yeah, got to pee?" Purdy grinned and walked on. Other girls and boys shouted at him, "Got to pee?" and "Don't pee." Purdy only smiled. He knew the school was prone to impromptu celebrations of this sort. One day it had been "wazzup" day, and everyone in the school greeted each other with "wazzup?" and sprinkled the word liberally into their conversations. On another occasion, students answered every question with, "I'm not a doctor." This especially infuriated some teachers. "Jimmy," the teacher would say, "How many pints are there in a gallon?" "I'm not a doctor," came the reply. No one seemed responsible for starting these events, and they would end as abruptly and mysteriously as they began, like some mild form of mass hysteria. So, Purdy concluded as he reached his classroom, it must be "got to pee" day.

As he entered the room all his classmates turned toward him and shouted, "Got to pee?" and laughed. It was then he saw that the walls of the classroom were festooned with copies of the front page of that morning's "Weekly Sentinel," the town newspaper, which bore the headline, "Local Boy Foils Crime Spree." Below the headline was a photo of Purdy and Amar standing in front of the Stop 'N' Shop, shaking hands and smiling weakly in response to the directions of the newspaper photographer.

Purdy enjoyed a moment of pleasure at the recognition, then felt his stomach start to turn to stone as he realized that the "got to pee" remarks were about him. He slunk to his desk. Savitri looked up from the book she was reading, gave him a quick smile, and bent her head down to resume pretending to read. She had, he learned later, already been bombarded with questions about her father and his store. No, her father did not keep a gun under the counter. No, it was not dangerous to shop there. No, he was not going to hire a guard. "It's a convenience store," she had explained. "It's supposed to get robbed. It's no big deal. It's expected, like paying taxes."

"Settle down," admonished Mrs. Martinez. She picked up a copy of the newspaper from her desk. "Oh, what have we got here?" she said in mock surprise. "It seems to be an article about our town hero." She adjusted her glasses and began to read:

"A statewide spree of convenience store robberies was ended Tuesday afternoon thanks to the quick thinking of 12 year old Casi Nada resident Purdy Hooper..."

"Read our favorite part," interrupted Creighton, who did not wait, taking the task upon himself: *"When asked if he had been scared, Hooper confessed, 'Heck yeah, I thought I'd pee my pants.'"*

The class again broke into a chorus of laughter and shouts of "got to pee?" Purdy lowered his forehead slowly onto his desktop and considered how nice it would be if a giant comet should choose that particular moment to slam into the Earth.

"Hey, Hooper," shouted Creighton, "thought you might need this." He pulled a disposable diaper from his desk and threw it at Purdy. The volume of shouts and cheers caused teachers in other classrooms to peer out their doors and exchange angry glances.

Purdy picked the diaper up off the floor and said, "I wouldn't want to leave you one short," and tossed it back. The laughter and shouting were aimed at Creighton now, who glowered, stuffing the diaper back into his desk.

This was going to be a day, Purdy soon realized, like so many other days, that would simply have to be endured. "One foot after the other," he told himself, which was part of a little pep talk he had devised for himself years earlier when he was still living in Phoenix. He had missed the school bus home one day and decided to walk home. The walk turned out to be much longer than he had supposed it to be from his bus rider's perspective. As he trudged through the afternoon heat and wondered if he would make it, he urged himself on, saying, "just put one foot after the other. That's not so much to do. One foot after the other."

<>

After lunch, his digestive system informed him that the tensions of the day were about to be released in a very material way, and he walked rather quickly to the boy's bathroom, constructed a hasty nest of toilet paper in one of the stalls, and sat down. When a few productive minutes of contemplation had passed he reached down to pull up his pants, but another pair of hands reached under the stall, grabbed them, and began pulling them, and him, out.

"Hey!" Purdy shouted. "Stop that! Hey!" He felt his shoes being pried off. "Stop!" He was clinging to the side of the toilet with one hand to prevent being pulled to the ground, and holding on to his pants with the other. With a sudden snap he saw his pants and underwear disappear under the stall door. In his fury all he could manage to say was, "Hey! Hey!" A disposable diaper dropped over the top of the stall and landed at his feet. A moment later he heard Creighton's laughter and the sound of the bathroom door swinging shut.

Purdy did not, would not, use obscene language. It annoyed him to hear other kids cursing, and, as best he could, he tried to avoid observing in himself those behaviors that annoyed him in others. From time to time he would use junior curses, such as "gosh darn," sanitized, diluted versions of the real thing. More and more, however, he was finding that the language he declined to use out loud was creeping into his internal monologue. And so, at this moment as he stood shoeless and half naked in a bathroom stall, a stream of invective flowed though his mind, curses which would impress a Marine.

He peered under the stall door and could see his shoes beneath the row of sinks, but no sign of his pants. He could hear that he was alone in the restroom so he poked his head out the door to look around. His pants were definitely gone. He looked at the diaper lying at his feet and angrily kicked it out of sight. He knew he would have to leave the bathroom half naked, and there was never any debate as to which half, so he took off his shirt and wrapped it, in as complete and unrevealing a manner as possible around his lower half. Then he put his shoes on and was about to leave when he recalled having watched the custodian changing the garbage bag in the trash can, lifting it out and then taking a new bag from the bottom of the can. Was that standard practice? Sure enough, when Purdy pulled the full bag out of the can he saw a shiny new black bag neatly folded at the bottom. He tore a hole in it and wore it like a poncho. Then, in a stiff, dignified march, his hands clamped to the makeshift kilt at front and behind, he strode out into the hallway. To the astonished students quietly staring at him he explained, "Peed my pants."

He sat in the nurse's office wearing a borrowed sweater, waiting for his pants to be located. He suspected that his cell phone would still be in his pocket, so he gave the school custodian his phone number. Calling Purdy's number on his own cell phone, the custodian listened for the ringing and soon located the missing pants and underwear. They were adorning the heads of the large busts of Washington and Lincoln that sat in nooks on either side of the entrance to the school's auditorium. Creighton was not a student of bully history or he would have known that the proper place for displaying stolen pants was up a flagpole.

The nurse, and then the principal asked Purdy who had taken his pants, but he lied and said he didn't know. Had he gotten Creighton in trouble now, he knew the trouble would not last and Creighton would return and revenge himself. Instead, he would let Creighton know that he could get him expelled at any time, which would keep him in check while Purdy plotted, slowly, and with relish, his own revenge.

<>

10

It had been a bad, bad day, and no choir of angels could have sounded sweeter to Purdy's ears than did the 3:00 dismissal bell. One chore still lay between him and the solitude and safety of his little bedroom. His mother had made him promise to deliver a thank you note to Amar.

"But the basket was a thank you," Purdy had objected. "You don't send a thank you for a thank you."

"It was a thank you," Doreen agreed, "but it was also a gift, and a gift must be noticed proper. You don't send a thank you and people would think you didn't like the gift, or didn't appreciate it, or that you're a selfish s.o.b. and think you deserve it. My momma used to say…"

"Oh, jeez, did you have to listen to everything your momma told you? You think I do?"

"I know you don't," Doreen said, "but you're gonna this time."

As his bicycle approached the Stop 'N' Shop, which was already being referred to in town as the Stop 'N' Rob, Purdy noticed that the small parking lot was packed full of cars. He had never seen more than three cars parked there at a time, so wondered if some new incident had just occurred. He pushed the door open cautiously. Amar saw him and came around the counter to meet him.

"Purdy, my friend," he said, patting him on the shoulders. "Look at this crowd. Isn't it wonderful? It's been like this all day. We should get almost robbed every week." He went back behind the counter to point out the framed copy of the newspaper article which he had hung on the back wall behind the cash register, in a spot where a faded beer advertisement had been. Purdy handed over his note, and additional thank yous were exchanged.

Once outside, Purdy discovered that the front tire of his bicycle had gone flat. "Perfect," he said aloud, "just perfect. What more can happen today?"

"I give up," came Joe's voice. "What?"

"Joe, where have you been?" Purdy said angrily. "You are never around when I need you."

"Why, what happened today?"

"I don't want to talk about it."

"Well, you brought it up, so maybe you do want to talk about it," said Joe.

"No. When I said, 'I don't want to talk about it,' that was a little hint that I don't want to talk about it." He walked his bicycle around the back of the store and onto the unpaved desert road that was a shortcut to his home. After a minute he stopped to inspect half of a rabbit, the back half, that was lying in the roadway. "I'd guess a housecat did this," he said.

"Could be a coyote," said Joe.

"Nah, a coyote wouldn't have left any." With his foot he pushed the hindquarters of the rabbit off to the side of the road, and covered it with a few big rocks.

"A burial?" said Joe.

"I guess." Addressing the mound he said, "Rest in peace, half a bunny," and turned away. "Hey, Joe, do you think heaven is like where you are? Like Sockworld?"

"In what way?"

Like maybe it's another layer of the world we can't see."

"Hmm, I'd have to say it doesn't seem likely," said Joe, as they continued walking, "but I'd have said Sockworld doesn't seem likely either, before I got here. Some of the other people here have mentioned that there is another door – that's how they put it – another door, but I don't know exactly what they are talking about. I never saw it."

They became aware of the sound of a pickup truck coming up the road behind them, and Purdy moved off to the left to let it pass. The truck slowed to match the speed of Purdy's walking, and the driver, a young man, peered at him from beneath the shade of a black baseball cap.

"Howdy," said Purdy.

The young man nodded. "You're the one, right?"

"What?"

"You're that hero kid from the paper."

"No, not me," Purdy lied.

"Yeah, you're the one. The paper said you got red hair."

"All redheads look alike."

"No, no, you're the one. I see your bike is busted. Let me give you a lift."

"No, thanks." He noticed a tattoo on the man's neck. It was black barbed wire, and it seemed to creep up from under his shirt like dead ivy.

The truck stopped. Purdy quickened his pace. "Thanks," he called back. "Can't take rides from strangers."

"I ain't a stranger," the man said, getting out of the truck. "You know my brother."

Joe said, "He has a tattoo. The tattoo. The truck. Run Purdy!"

Purdy dropped his bicycle and began to run through the desert. He did not get far before the young man grabbed his collar and spun him around.

"Let me go," yelled Purdy.

"My brother's in jail now, but he said if I were to ever meet you I should treat you real special. Let's get in the truck."

"Joe, help me!"

"Who's Joe?" said the man.

Joe said loudly, "Let him go! Let him go! Let him go!"

"Not helping," said Purdy, but Joe continued to repeat "Let him go. Let him go."

Purdy felt something buzzing near his face and lifted his hand to brush it away. Out of the palm of his raised hand a man's fist appeared in the air and punched the young man in the nose, and then disappeared. The young man fell straight back and lay unconscious on the ground, blood dripping from his nose.

"Whoa!" said Purdy. "I didn't know you could do that."

"Me neither," said Joe. "I felt it. I really felt it. I was almost out for a moment."

"Well, what were you doing?"

"I was punching him through his head. I kept punching and punching," said Joe, "thinking maybe I could create some electrical disturbance in his brain."

"Wow, cool!" said Purdy. "You sure did. Do it again. Maybe you can get all the way out." He could hear Joe's grunts as he punched.

"It's no good," said Joe. "Something was different. I don't know what. Anyway, we don't have much time. He won't be out forever. Look in his truck and see if you can find something to tie him up with."

Purdy emerged from the truck with a roll of duct-tape.

"Great," said Joe. "Roll him over and tie his hands and feet together."

Purdy worked quickly and when he was done he threw his hands in the air the way he had seen cowboys in rodeos do when they were done roping a calf.

"Good job! Now check his pockets, see if he has a wallet."

"Oh, yeah," said Purdy. "So we can see his i.d." He pulled a wallet from the man's pocket.

"No. We know who he is. He's that robber's brother. It's to see if he has any money."

Purdy dropped the wallet. "No way. I'm not going to rob him."

"He was going to kill you, most likely. It's more than fair. If he has money it's probably stolen anyway. He didn't earn it."

"No," said Purdy. "I wouldn't feel right. What if he told the police I robbed him?"

"OK, first of all, no man is going to admit to being beat up by a little kid. Second, if his money is missing, he'll assume the police took it."

"Still…" He bent down and looked in the wallet. "There's like three hundred dollars in here."

"OK, Purdy, look at it this way. Do it for your mom. Think how hard she works and never gets ahead. Give it to her."

"She would never take it."

"You're smart. You'll find a way."

Purdy sighed, stuffed the money in his back pocket, then put the wallet back in the man's pants. "Sometimes I don't know about you, Joe." His cell phone rang. His heart raced a moment as his first thought was that the sheriff somehow knew he had stolen money and was calling. He exhaled in relief when he saw his mom's phone number show up. "Hi, mom. Oh, yeah, sorry I forgot to call. Yeah, everything's fine. OK, see you later. Love you too." He put the phone back in his pocket. "She worries too much," he said.

11

Purdy broke off a branch of a bush locals called "Indian Scrub Brush," and swept away all his sneaker and bicycle tracks. He retraced his path back to the Stop 'N' Shop, sweeping all the way. He wanted no publicity this time. Disguising his voice on the payphone, he made an anonymous call to the Sheriff's office, telling them there was a mysterious package tied up on the desert road. Later that week he read in the paper that a third member of the gang that had been robbing convenience stores had been captured. The robber had been found tied up in the desert and claimed he had been beaten by a group of men, though, curiously, the authorities noted that his truck had not been stolen.

When Purdy finally arrived home he let his bicycle drop and sat wearily on the front steps. "Thanks again, Joe," he said. "You saved my life."

"Glad I could help, though I still don't know how I did it. I've been punching ever since but nothing happens."

"At least you know it's possible now. Keep trying."

"I will."

"It's all so weird," said Purdy. "The tattoo, the truck, the kidnapping attempt. Guess your dream came true after all."

"Didn't I say it would?" said Joe.

"Yeah. I won't make fun of your predictions anymore."

"Of course you will."

"Is that a prediction?" Purdy laughed. "Guess you're right. See you later… well, you know what I mean." He went inside and plopped down on his bed, wanting nothing more than to take a nap, but the events of the day kept playing over and over in his mind and would not let him sleep.

Later, during dinner, Purdy could barely keep his eyes open. Once he had cleared the table he announced to his mother that he was going to bed early.

"Feeling OK?" asked Doreen.

"Sure. It's just been a long day. A long week."

"It has," she agreed. "Leastways tomorrow's Saturday. You can sleep late. Night Darlin'."

<>

Purdy, standing before his bed, had stripped down to his underwear and was about to put on his pajamas when he felt a dizzy spell come upon him. Always before he had fought against this feeling, but now he felt too tired to fight, so rather than resisting the dizzy feeling he leaned into it. He fell backwards onto his bed but the bed did not stop his fall. He fell through the bed and tumbled over and over before finally righting himself. Once again he was standing where he had started. "What a weird dream," he thought. Looking down, he was surprised to see that his feet were hovering five inches above the ground. He lifted one foot to see what he was standing on and his entire body floated higher off the ground. Afraid he would hit the ceiling he tried to move down, and his body complied. He thought himself to the right and he moved right. He thought himself to the left and moved left. He had soon mastered the controls of this balloon-like dream body. He spun and dove all around the room, like a bird that had flown in through an open window and didn't know how to get out. Miscalculating, he flew into his desk, but rather than knocking the desk over he passed right through it. The desk appeared solid enough, although he now noticed that objects did appear to shimmer slightly. He plunged his hand through the desk again. He could see the desk but could not touch it.

As he stopped to consider this new information he saw a black object floating across the room towards him. He backed up, fearing it was a bat, though he quickly realized it was moving too slow and straight to be a bat. He then saw that it was a black sock, which placidly floated by him and disappeared into the opposite wall.

"I'm not dreaming," he exclaimed, "I'm in Sockworld." He looked around, thinking he might see Joe, but found he was still alone in his room. "Joe," he called. There was no reply. How had he gotten here, and why? He did not know. It all seemed so impossible that he returned to his first hypothesis, that he was asleep and dreaming. How could he be sure he was awake? He dipped his toe into that philosophical nightmare and withdrew. "No," he concluded, "That's not something I've ever asked myself in a dream. That only happens in bad movies – 'It was all a dream. Ha, ha.' – Grrr. No." He concluded he was definitely awake and had somehow slipped into Sockworld.

During his pondering he had been pacing the floor, though his feet were not touching the ground. His next thought was to show his mom how he could fly. He moved to the door and grasped at the doorknob but his hand kept passing right through it. "How am I going to get out" he thought. "Oh, right." He pushed his hand through the door a few times to test it, and then he backed up, lowered his head, and commanded himself forward. He plunged through the door and down the short hallway into the living room.

Doreen was curled up on the couch watching a TV show about Italian cooking. Purdy hovered between her and the television. "Mom, look," he said, turning a somersault in the air. "Mama?" She continued watching TV right through him, neither seeing nor hearing him. Purdy moved closer, waving his hand before her eyes. "Mama," he shouted.

In a panic he began spinning around the room, faster and faster. On the fourth spin he shot through the front wall of the trailer and out into the night. It was a cloudless dark night. Out in the front yard, although he could not feel the cold night air, he began to shiver. "Oh my gosh. Oh my gosh. What if she can never see me again? She's already lost my Dad. She couldn't stand losing me too. I couldn't stand it. Oh my gosh, am I stuck here forever?"

"Think," he commanded himself. "Calm down. Think. Think, think, think, think, think. How did I get in? What was I doing? OK, OK, I was in my room, getting undressed. I started to get a dizzy spell. A dizzy… could that be it? Is it like a spell, a trance? Dizzy? Is that the key? I can do that. I can do that." He concentrated on the place in his forehead where his dizzy spells seemed centered and began to bring on that spinning feeling. In an instant he felt the cold breeze, and the sharp gravel of the front yard biting into his bare knees. "Ouch!" He laughed. "I'm back. I did it."

He started to get up when a car turning a corner flashed its headlights across his yard. He crouched down, suddenly realizing he was outside wearing only a pair of white briefs. Still crouching, he crept up the front stairs and grasped the door handle. Locked. With a sigh he knocked on the door. His mother pulled aside the curtains and peered out.

"Purdy," she said. "Good Lord, you gave me a start. What in the world are you doing outside in your skivvies?"

"Could we maybe discuss this in the house?" Purdy said. The door lock clicked and he slipped inside. He ran to his room and crashed into the door, falling back onto the carpet, having forgotten that he could no longer pass through the door as he had on the way out.

Purdy," his mother exclaimed. "What in Heaven's name? Are you OK?"

"I'm fine." He laughed, rubbing his nose.

"You're not doing drugs, are you?"

"No!" He got up, opened his door and put on a bathrobe.

"Well?"

"I don't know," said Purdy. "I think I must have been sleepwalking."

Doreen was visibly relieved. "Sleepwalking. Yes, that must have been it. You never did that before. I don't remember any sleepwalkers in my family. Well, my cousin Jacob, but he always woke up somewhere across town smelling like beer so his mama had her 'spicions. Maybe on your Daddies' side. Guess we'll have to tie a bell on you."

"Guess so. Sorry to scare you." He gave her a hug and while he did he could tell she was sniffing his breath.

Back in his room he started to put on his pajamas again, and did so quickly, a little afraid that it was part of the process that would send him back into Sockworld. Once he had his pajamas on without event he exhaled in relief.

"Man, I'm never doing that again," he said to himself, knowing even as he said it that he certainly would.

12

For the next week Purdy tried to keep himself extra busy while he pretended that nothing had happened. He worked on extra credit assignments at school, though his grades were always perfect. At home he did chores that his mother hadn't requested. It was harder to keep busy on the weekend and by the next Sunday he found the pretense unsustainable. As he munched on a slightly burned toaster waffle, Purdy turned at last to the problem he had avoided, seeking in vain for a reason not to visit Sockworld again. It seemed safe enough since he knew he could get out again. Flying was undeniably cool. Having been in Sockworld only a few minutes had already rendered the real world less permanent and comforting. If the solid Earth and all its objects could in an instant be as soluble as smoke, what did solid mean? If his own living body, as real to him as anything, could also be invisible and silent as a ghost, what was real? He knew so much less than he had just days before. His first visit to Sockworld had been like riding the biggest, fastest roller-coaster in the world. It scared him, in his own sanitized version of the phrase, spitless, but he was twelve, so that only meant he had to ride it again.

He thought that maybe he would wait until Joe showed up, and then pop into his world with a flourish. He had even scripted the moment. "Hey Joe," he would say, "Wanna see a magic trick? Abra Cadabra!" He wondered, however, if that might hurt Joe's feelings. Joe considered Sockworld a prison. Would it be rude to pop in and out of Sockworld with ease when Joe was stuck there? No, he decided he would explore Sockworld a while on his own before telling Joe of his new-found ability.

To start, he stood in his room and made a few quick test flights into Sockworld and back out again, to convince himself he would not get stuck there. He moved back and forth from visible to invisible almost instantaneously. It was as if that that area in his forehead was a switch he had often seen but never tried because he didn't know what it was for. Now that he knew he flipped it on and off as if he had always used it. Satisfied of his ability to return home he closed his eyes and shot up through the roof. Doors were for the Earthbound. Ceilings and walls were the passageways of Sockworld. He paused a few moments looking down at his trailer park. There were many fenced-in yards he had never seen before. A few people were out and about but no one noticed him hovering above, no dog barked. He observed that he didn't cast a shadow.

He flew low over the whole town, passing over the church, the junkyard, the glass factory, the gas stations and restaurants by the highway. His school was closed for the weekend, but there were a few teenagers out back playing basketball. He flew over the supermarket where his mom was working and dove down through the roof to see her in action. She was a really good checker, quick but friendly. She knew everyone in Casi Nada, and most of the people from neighboring towns that didn't have a supermarket. She smiled at everyone, but he also noticed how tired she looked. It suddenly felt as if he were spying on her, so he ascended again.

He settled down onto Main Street, standing, in so far as he could be considered to stand, in the middle of the road. A small red car was coming toward him. He waited until it was only inches away then hopped over it. "Yee haw!" he shouted, laughing. He had invented a new game – car hopping. He waited for the next car. "Yahoo!" The next car was a large, refrigerated truck. "OK, big guy. You think you've got what it takes to beat the Purdinator?" Purdy taunted. "Bring it." He leapt at the last moment. "Yippee!" He laughed and turned to watch the vanquished enemy run away. As he watched there was a sudden flash of metal and bodies. Another car he hadn't noticed had come up from behind and passed right through him.

"Whoa," Purdy exclaimed. He was shaken at first, but then laughed at himself for his own concern. He saw another car approaching. Could he do it – let it run right through him? He waited, waited, then leapt. "Darn," he said. "OK, OK, I wasn't ready. OK, here comes another one." He waited, waited, then leapt again. "Darn!" Although he knew the cars could not hurt him it was not an easy thing to keep from leaping out of the way of an oncoming vehicle.

"OK, I've got this," he told himself. "Come on," he shouted at the approaching pickup truck. "Come on! Come Aaaaah!" The engine, the windshield, the driver's face, the back window, the bed full of lumber all flashed by. "Aaaaah!" Purdy kept screaming until the scream turned into laughter.

He rose into the air, turned, and flew very fast until he had caught up to the truck that had just passed through him. Travelling alongside, Purdy peered in at the oblivious driver. Speeding up, he passed the truck, and then the next two cars ahead. Although he was moving very quickly, he had no real sensation of speed. No wind blew in his face or buzzed in his ears. Forty miles an hour did not feel much different than five. How fast could he go, he wondered.

Purdy zoomed ahead and the town was gone in moments. Below him flashed desert, and then colorful squares of farmland, and then vacant desert again. Urging himself faster, even the desert blurred beneath him. He realized he had begun to spin, and slowed to a stop. He found himself on the bank of a dry stream bed. In the distance, a dust devil, like a miniature tornado, kicked up dust and debris as it twirled in a drunken line across the flat landscape. Purdy could not see anything familiar in any direction.

Fueled by panic, he shot up into the sky, much higher than he had previously dared, in hopes that this vantage point would show him the way home. Still he viewed anonymous desert all around. Then, flying twenty feet beneath him, he saw three socks. Two black socks and one white sock were flying in a V shaped formation. His eye followed the direction of this flying arrow and it was then that he saw, much further away than he though possible, the tiny snake of highway and small chip of white that was the Catholic church, the tallest building in his small town. He estimated that Casi Nada was thirty miles away from him. Could he have gone that far in only a minute? He did the math in his head. Thirty miles a minute times sixty minutes: eighteen hundred miles an hour. Joe had said he could fly faster than a plane, but until now Purdy had never really considered what that meant.

Flying back toward town at a more leisurely pace than he had flown away from it, Purdy had time to think about that odd goose V of socks. What a strange coincidence that they were out there in the middle of nowhere pointing in the direction of town. What if it wasn't coincidence? Did Sockworld somehow know where he wanted to go and send him a sign to help him? That was just too many impossible things even for this improbable place.

13

As he flew over the highway toward town, Purdy decided to hitch a ride. He dove into a small blue car. The driver, a man in his thirties, with a shaved head to disguise his baldness under more baldness, was alone in the car, yet he was talking aloud and waving his free hand. It was then Purdy noticed the cell phone receiver in the man's ear.

"Right," said the man, unaware of Purdy hovering beside him, "So, I said, 'What do you mean spots are extra.' Right. So he says, 'Spots are extra.' Right. So I say, 'Why the hell would I need my carpet cleaned it if didn't have spots?' I know, right?"

Purdy shot out the side of the car and into a silver car heading the other direction. A middle-aged woman was driving and an old woman sat beside her. The back seat was piled high with suitcases.

"I hope you're going to behave yourself when we get to the airport," said the driver.

"Who am I?" the old woman shrugged.

"Ma, you know what I'm talking about. Last time we nearly missed our flight."

"I wish I should go already," said the old woman.

"Shut up. Don't talk that way. Just don't make no comments."

"What did I say?"

"You know what you said. They were patting you down and you said, 'You think I'm a terrorist? Maybe I got a bomb up my butt?'"

"They were touching my panties."

"I don't care. You can't make terrorist jokes at the airport. They got no sense of humor. Just keep quiet."

The old woman shook her head. "I wish you should just put me on an iceberg and let me float out to sea."

"Shut up, Ma. Don't talk that way. Everyone loves you."

Purdy rose up through the roof. The thrill of eavesdropping had dissipated much more quickly than he could have imagined. He was beginning to feel tired, so he turned and flew directly home, reappearing in his bedroom. The first thing he felt upon re-entry was the thud of gravity, a feeling like being in a falling elevator that stops too quickly. The second, and more surprising thing he experienced was a whoosh of smells. Sockworld had been devoid of scents, though he had not noticed their absence. Now he could smell everything – pencil shavings, the detergent in his clothes, the wet sand in his crab's tank ("Have to change that," he noted). Usually, while he would smell good smells, like warm bread or bacon cooking, or bad smells, like fertilizer or perfume, he was, for the majority of his day, not consciously aware of any smells at all. Now, for a few minutes, until the ability faded, he was a bloodhound. Something beckoned to him from the kitchen. His mom, who was not home, though he could still detect her shampoo, had left a small jar of cinnamon uncovered. To Purdy, the spice blared like a boom box.

After a snack, he returned to his room and took an unused spiral notebook from his desk drawer. On the first page he wrote, "Purdy's Top Secret Journal." While he meant it to be secret, it was only "top secret" because that sounded cool. It was a journal rather than a diary because he thought a diary was more of a girl thing, and also because diary sounded close to how his mother pronounced "dairy." He could imagine his mom discovering the notebook and exclaiming, "Purdy has top secret dairy? So that's where all the cheese is disappearing to."

Though he had written journals before, he decided to write a top secret journal now because, for the first time in his life, he actually had a huge secret. He had not told his mom about Joe or Sockworld yet. Now he was invisibly flying around the town and beyond. That was huge, and he yearned to share it with someone. With no siblings or close friends he had lived a very solitary childhood, and for him writing often took the place of talking. Two years earlier everyone in his class had received a letter from an international pen-pal. Purdy received a one paragraph letter from a boy in England.

"Dear Pen Friend,
My name is Jeremy. I am ten years old. I am mad for football and Space Monkeys (a video game). I have a cat and a sister. What do you like?
Sincerely,
Jeremy"

Purdy replied with a typewritten letter that was eight pages long. Jeremy never wrote back.

After debating the merits of creating a secret code in which to write his top secret journal, Purdy decided English would suffice for the moment. He could always transcribe it into code later. He recorded all the details of his trip into Sockworld that morning. Then, as there was nothing good on TV he decided to go back to Sockworld so he would have more to write about.

He shot up through the roof. He still had not seen Joe, and wondered where he went when he was gone for days. "I'll have to remember to ask him," he decided. "Fast as you can go here, he could be anywhere in the world." Purdy thought about all the places he might travel – the beach, Disneyland, Dinosaur National Monument, Africa, Stonehenge, Machu Pichu. Recalling his panic when he found himself far from town that morning, he knew he would not attempt any long trips until he figured out a sure method of finding his way back. He could not always depend on a serendipitous trio of socks passing by.

Having no plan of where to go, he followed the familiar paths he would have taken had he been on his bicycle. Arriving at the town's Main Street he rose to a height of ten feet so he would not have to avoid flying through people. It did not hurt to do so, but the idea of it did not appeal to him.

Several feet above him he noticed a small bird, but it was not flying. It was slowly floating down toward him. Excited to see another living occupant of Sockworld, Purdy flew up beside it. The small mourning dove lay tilted to one side. "Is it dead?" Purdy wondered. "Is there death here?" This had not occurred to him before. Up until then he had considered Sockworld to be a big, safe playground where nothing could hurt him. If there was death, was there pain as well? Suffering there certainly was, as Joe had attested. To its living occupants, Sockworld was a prison. It was as if Purdy had discovered shards of glass amid the playground gravel.

He cupped the bird in his hands. To say he touched it would be inaccurate, as neither he nor the bird had a physical presence here. His hands did not pass through the bird, however. The bird's space and his own were inviolate. Cupping the bird in his hands felt like clamping onto it with very weak magnets. This, he decided later, would be called "clitching," a word he made up which meant connecting without touching.

The bird woke, and then shifted its wings. Purdy took his hands away. The dove did not fly away at once. It tilted its small gray head to look at Purdy, made a low trilling sound, then floated off several feet and looked back. It looked up and then quickly disappeared into the distance.
A shadow crossed the sun.

14

Looking up, Purdy saw a red-tailed hawk circling high above. "So that's what scared off the dove. It must know by now that the hawk can't see it here. Guess instinct is hard to argue with." He rose up and flew alongside the hawk. He had seen hawks all his life, but never one so close before. He marveled at how little effort it took for the hawk to fly so high. Riding the updraft of hot air over the highway it did not flap a wing, did not move a muscle. The only parts of it that moved were its beautiful, terrible amber eyes. It was, Purdy decided, the most perfectly designed living machine. If there was such a thing as reincarnation, he put in his vote to come back as a hawk. The diet of mostly rodents, lizards, and small birds didn't appeal to him, but he supposed they would be pizza and ice cream to him were he a hawk.

Purdy was not as patient as a hawk so after fifteen minutes of circling he flew slowly back down into town. Glancing back, he was surprised to see another large black bird that seemed to be following him. As it grew larger and larger the ancient dove portion of Purdy's brain became apprehensive. He stood his ground, however, his ground being a bit of space above the Laundromat.

Before long he realized it was not a bird at all but an old woman with an enormous black cape. When she came to a stop in front of him he could see that the cape was made up of hundreds of black socks. The woman regarded him through squinted eyes. She had long white hair pulled back tight, and every angle of her face – nose, cheekbones, chin – seemed honed to a point.

"Hello," said Purdy.

"Bonjour," squeaked the woman. "Parlez vouz Francais?"

"Oh, great," thought Purdy. "I finally meet someone in Sockworld and she doesn't speak English." He shook his head. "No," he said. "Not much. Un petit."

"Pity. Well, Mort, you have taken your time getting here. I've been waiting."

"I'm sorry, I think you're mistaking me for somebody else. My name's not Mort. My name is Purdy."

"Ah," said the woman. "Short for perdition. I've been waiting for you for twenty years."

"See, it couldn't be me because…"

"Are you telling me I don't know what I'm talking about?" the woman snapped.

"No, Ma'am."

"It is pronounced 'madam,' not 'ma'am.' I always tell my students, 'don't sound like a sheep. Ma'am! It is madam. We are not cowboys, oui?"

"Oui. But you see I'm only 12."

"Yes, so?"

"So," said Purdy, "how could you be waiting for me for twenty years if I'm only 12?"

"Ah, but how many years have you been 12?"

Purdy realized that talking about time here could be complicated, and gave up arguing. "So, you said something about students. You're a teacher?"

"I was a teacher, before…"

"Before what?

"Before I died, of course. I was Madam Silvia Bruneau, teacher of French to idiots. I taught at Cholla High School in Tucson for thirty years. A more thankless task there never was. So close to Mexico, who would want to learn Francais, French? But year after year they came, to murder my beautiful language. Baudelaire is still spinning in his grave."

Purdy began to float nervously back and forth. "OK, hold on," he said. "Back up, rewind, do not pass go. You… you think you're dead?"

"Does this look like living?" Madame Bruneau said, and threw her arms wide so forcefully that she lost a few sock from her cape. They flew away a few feet and then slowly returned to their places.

Purdy had to admit to himself that it did not look like living at all. Down below in the street he could see people, noisy, solid, walking on the ground. Had Joe lied? Was Joe dead? Was everyone here dead? No, not everyone. He knew he was alive. The only difference he could see between himself and Madame Bruneau was that he could leave and she could not. He imagined her waking up here one day and finding that everyone she knew could no longer see her, hear her, feel her. Watching year after year as the world went on, forgetting about her. Thinking herself to be dead was the most reasonable conclusion she could have reached. He could tell her that she was mistaken, that she was not dead but only stuck here, but what good would that do? If she believed him it would only make her sadder.

"So, will you take me the rest of the way now?" asked Madam Bruneau.

"What?"

"How long must I wait?"

"Um, I'm sorry, I don't know," said Purdy. He had no idea what she was talking about.

"So long," she wailed. "I have waited so long. So many wait. Even the old king, how he suffers, poor creature. Will it be soon?"

"I…" Purdy wanted to explain again that he was only 12 years old but was interrupted.

"Say maybe," said Madam Bruneau, clitching her hand to his sleeve. "Maybe, and you lighten my heart. Maybe and you do not crush my hopes to dust."

Purdy did not know what he was committing himself to, but 'maybe' seemed safe enough so he said it. "Maybe."

"Merci!" she shouted, and threw her cape into the air. It burst apart, socks flying in every direction. Then she raised her hands and the socks swarmed back, once again forming a cape around her shoulders. "I must tell the others."

"No, wait," said Purdy, but she was far out of sight in moments. "Man, she was kind of weird," he said to himself, "even for a teacher."

He decided to look around some of the shops as long as he was here. First he had to find a secluded place where he could appear. The alley behind the shops might do, but when he got there he was annoyed to find a child sitting beside a dumpster, crying. He looked around, and then appeared on the opposite side of the dumpster.

"Hey," said Purdy.

"Hey," said the crying girl. She appeared to be five or six, and was seated on a collapsed cardboard box, alongside a bottle of water, a box of cheese crackers, and a doll. Purdy noticed a string running from a loop of her pants to the dumpster.

"Who tied you here?" he asked.

The child pointed toward the back door of one of the shops. "My mom has to work."

"Oh. Does she always tie you here?"

"No, but she couldn't find a babysitter."

"Oh, sure," said Purdy. "Would you run away if you weren't tied up?"

The girl shook her head no. Purdy looked around and found a broken piece of a bottle. He used it to cut the rope at the dumpster end. "There," he said, "you're not a dog, after all. You OK? What are you crying about?"

"I'm cold."

It was not cold. It was late September and the temperature was still in the high nineties. Purdy felt the girl's forehead. She seemed fine. He decided she must be talking about a lonely kind of cold. "Oh, it is kind of shady. OK, no problem. There's a thrift store right around here. I'll get you a little jacket or something. I'll be right back, OK?"

When Purdy reached the thrift store he saw in the reflection of the glass door that the girl was right behind him.

"Hey," he said, "you said you wouldn't run away."

"I'll go back," said the girl, pushing past him.

"Oh, all right. See that corner back there? That's the kid's corner. Go pick out a coat or sweater. I'll be looking around."

After a short time the girl reappeared. "I want this," she said, holding up a small Scooby Doo blanket.

"Don't you want a coat?"

"I want this."

"OK. You like Scooby Doo? I don't. It's never a real ghost or monster. Never." The price tag was marked a dollar fifty, but as it was Sunday everything was half price. He paid for the blanket as well as an old tin canister he had found with a fifty dollar bill, and got forty nine dollars back. Borrowing a pen from the attendant he wrote a note on the back of one of the thrift store fliers.

"Here," he said to the girl once they got outside, "give this note to your mom if she asks where you got the blanket from."

"OK."

He watched the girl toddle happily back to the alley wrapped in her blanket. The note said, "Blanket courtesy of the Mother of the Year Selection Committee."

<>

15

After a day of flying around Sockworld, school seemed more confining than ever. Purdy was looking forward to his computer lab class, however. His mom could not afford internet access at home so this was his chance to google Madam Bruneau and see when she disappeared. When he did search her name he didn't find anything about her. She had mentioned an old king. Surely if a king was missing that would be in the news, but Purdy's search turned up nothing but articles about people missing Elvis. In frustration, he typed in the question, *"What is the biggest waste of time?"* to see if the internet would name itself. The internet had not yet reached that level of self awareness, though, and served up articles about drugs, television, dieting, and Congress.

"Hello Purdy," came Joe's familiar voice. "How are you doing?"

Purdy was startled. Should he tell Joe that he could enter Sockworld? Should he show him? Something told him to wait. "Oh, hey Joe, where have you been all weekend? I wanted to see, I mean, talk to you."

"Oh, sorry. There was a conference on physics at the university in Tucson that I wanted to attend."

"How was it?"

"Over my head, mostly," said Joe.

Another student sat beside Purdy so he switched to a blank document on his computer and typed his response. "You can go to any concert, ballgame, movie, and you go to a physics lecture? You're just a party animal."

Joe laughed. "Well, I do go to shows sometimes. I saw the Stones the last time they played Phoenix."

"No, no seat at all. I was on stage with them. They were even older looking up close. So, what did you want to talk about?"

"Oh, nothing special," Purdy typed. "Just talk."

"OK, I'll drop by later when you're alone. Have fun."

After computer lab Purdy went back to his homeroom for his English class. Savitri was already in her seat, busily working on math problems.

"Hey, Savitri."

"Hey," she replied without looking up.

"Did you have to work this weekend?"

"A little. I don't mind."

Purdy glanced at the paper she was working on. "We doing math in English class now? The second problem is wrong."

"Shut up."

"No, really."

"Like you can do Algebra upside down?"

"I guess."

"What is that?" said Savitri. "One of the competitions in the Nerd Olympics?"

"Just helping."

"I don't need help."

"Aren't you going to fix it?"

Savitri turned her paper over. "Just mind your own business, stalker."

"I am not a stalker."

"Then why are you still looking at me? Stalker."

Purdy turned away. It occurred to him that he was now perfectly equipped to be a stalker. To mess with Savitri he decided he would go into Sockworld at lunchtime and follow her around, and later tell her something she did that he could not possibly know. When lunch break arrived he found an empty classroom and disappeared into Sockworld. Then he flew through the halls, high above the heads of the students, searching for Savitri.

He soon found her, huddling in a corner with Creighton. She was standing closer to him than Purdy thought necessary, and they were whispering.

"Are they all right?" asked Creighton.

"Yes," said Savitri, handing him a paper. "Mostly."

"Mostly? I told you I wanted them all right this time."

"And I told you, if you get them all right the teacher won't think you did the work yourself."

"Are you calling me stupid?" said Creighton.

Savitri hesitated. "I'm not calling you…"

"Look, just get them all right next time." He grabbed Savitri by the shoulder, spun her around, and shoved her away. She walked away smiling. Before he could work out why Savitri was helping his arch enemy cheat, Creighton was joined by two other boys.

"Hey, why do we always see you hanging with that Mexican chick?" said Rod.

"She's not Mexican," said Creighton.

"My sister's Mexican," said Javier.

"Maybe that's because you're Mexican too, dimwatt," said Creighton.

"Oh yeah. Thank you Mr. Obvious," said Javier. "I meant she was born there."

"So what's up with you two?" said Rod. "You hot for her or something?"

"Hell no. Don't even like her. Sometimes she does my math homework for me."

"Sweet," Creighton's friends chimed in unison.

"And what do you do for her?" asked Rod.

"Shut your face. I don't do nothing for her. She bugs me. I'm going to dump that trash soon."

"Can you get her to do my math homework?" said Javier.

"You wouldn't want her to," said Creighton. "She gets stuff wrong."

"Oh, heck with that. I can get it wrong on my own. But I don't get why you don't like her. She's kind of pretty."

"Not my type," said Creighton. "I'm into blondes."

"Oh yeah," said Rod. "Must be from all those years of kissing your mirror." He ran before Creighton could hit him with the book he was holding.

Purdy was burning above. He was already angry with Creighton, but hearing him call Savitri "trash" pushed him to act. "Time for a little revenge," he said to himself.

He went back to the empty classroom and appeared, then made his way through the crowds until he was behind Creighton and his friends. He worked up his courage, reached out, and knocked the book out from under Creighton's arm. Creighton seemed to move in slow motion, first looking down at the book, and then turning.

"Oh, hey," said Purdy. "You dropped your book." Without waiting for a reply he turned and ran into the nearest empty classroom and instantly disappeared. He watched as Creighton burst through the door.

"You're so dead," Creighton shouted. He looked around. "No use hiding, Hooper. The windows don't open, and there's no back door." He looked under the teacher's desk, then crouched to look under the other desks in the room. Then he went to the back of the class and triumphantly threw open the supply closet. It was empty.

"Where the hell are you?" Creighton shouted. He kicked a few desks and then left the classroom.

Purdy appeared and stuck his head out the door. "Hey, looking for me?" he said. He closed the door and disappeared again, waiting for the fun to begin once more. Creighton entered shouting, "Dead, dead, dead!" He took the same route as before, first checking under the teacher's desk, then the supply closet. He put his hands on the windows to see if somehow one would open. Then he got on top of the teacher's desk to see if he could reach the ceiling tiles. Finally he left again, audibly growling.

Purdy thought to himself, "I really shouldn't do it again. It's just not right. OK, one last time." He stuck his head out the door and said, "Yoo hoo, birdbrain."

Creighton entered screaming, a wordless scream, something between the rebel yell and a lawnmower. He scanned the empty classroom, then, still screaming, took his arm and swept everything on top of the teacher's desk onto the ground. He swung around just in time to see the look of astonishment on the face of the principal who was standing in the doorway.

"What in the world?" said Mr. Hughes. He was a rotund man whose head seemed to emerge directly from his shoulders. He went from surprise to anger without any intermediate emotions. "Come with me young man."
He guided Creighton through the hallway with his hand firmly grasping the boy's collar.

Before they reached the school office they met Purdy coming from the opposite direction.

"Oh, hey Creighton," said Purdy. "I think you lost this book." He handed Creighton his textbook. Creighton's eyes were bulging and a vein stood out on his forehead.

"What do you say?" demanded Mr. Hughes.

"Thanks," said Creighton through gritted teeth.

<>

16

The news that Creighton had been suspended for a week for trashing a classroom spread quickly through the school. Purdy caught himself grinning all day. He had wanted to talk to Savitri about it, and about what he had seen and heard but he never got an opportunity. What Savitri did puzzled him, and he knew he would be bouncing theories off the walls of his brain all evening.

When he opened the front door of his home his mother called, "Purdy, at last. Come quick."

"What's the matter?"

Doreen pointed to a small tin canister sitting in the center of the kitchen table. "It's a tin can," said Purdy.

"I know that. Open it."

Purdy reached for the can then pulled his hand away. "Is something going to jump out at me, like those fake cans of peanut brittle?"

"No. Open it."

He pulled off the lid slowly and said, "Oh, wow." Then he turned the can over and a wad of money fell onto the table. "There must be two hundred dollars."

"Three hundred and fifty seven," said Doreen.

"Wow. Have you been saving a dollar a day or something?"

"Save?" Doreen snorted. "Who can save? I found it."

"Found it? Where?"

"You'll never guess. OK, I'll tell you." Doreen had entered her story-telling mode, so Purdy sat down, knowing it would take a while. "Well," she continued, "I went out to work on my garden this morning and there was a big ass weed growing smack in the middle of my marigolds. You ever wonder why it is that weeds grow like weeds? If vegetables grew that fast nobody in the world would be hungry. Maybe you can work on that for a science project?"

"I'll put it on my to-do list. So the weed?"

"Oh, yeah. So I got my little shovel to dig it out, 'cause you got to get the roots, and I hear a clink. I push away the dirt and there it was, an old tin can stuffed with money. Imagine."

"Exciting," said Purdy.

"It was. Well, you know how if you find a dollar on the ground you always look around for more?"

Purdy's eyes widened. "You didn't dig up the whole garden, did you?"

"No, no. I ain't as dumb as I look. You know how old Mr. Garfield next door is always out with his metal detector looking for change? Well, I borrowed the metal detector, but no clicks. That's the noise it makes. No more cans of money. But it was fun, like a treasure hunt. We ought to save up and get one of those metal detectors."

"You don't have to save up," said Purdy. "You've got this load of money."

"Oh, no," said Doreen, fingering the money tenderly. "It ain't mine to keep. I got to turn it in to the police."

"What?"

"It's somebody's money for sure. They'll be missing it."

"What? Hold on, hit the brakes, drop anchor. Whoa! Let me think about this for a minute." He started to spread the money out on the table, turning each bill face up. When he had them all spread out he began looking closely at each bill.

"What are you doing?"

"Wait, almost done," said Purdy. "Yes, yes, all right." He straightened up. "You can keep the money. Look, every dollar has the year it was printed. There's nothing here newer than 1990. Whoever buried this money did it a long time ago. They're long gone. They're not coming back for it."

"Let me see," said Doreen, looking a few of the bills. "You really think…"

"It's all yours."

Doreen was silent a few moments, then scooped up two handfuls of money and threw them in
the air. "Yippee!"

Purdy had anticipated his mother's honesty, anticipated that she would want to turn in the money, the same money he had stolen for the kidnapper in the desert, so he had spent part of his weekend going from store to store trading new bills for old ones. It was his luck to live in a poor town, for poor people deal mostly in cash. As times had been harder than usual, lots of old cash had been flowing out of hiding places in mattresses, behind picture frames, and in freezers, so old bills were not too hard to find. He placed the new old money in the thrift store canister, and buried it in his mother's garden, planting a big weed over it to hasten its discovery.

As Purdy bent to pick up the money, Doreen sat down at the table, put her chin in her hand and stared into space. "I never even win the lottery," she said. "What should we do with it? I know you'd like to buy more books. Maybe I can get you some of them fancy sneakers. You do without so much."

"I don't need anything," said Purdy, returning the last of the bills to the table. "Get yourself something nice. You work so…"

"Ooh, ooh, I know," Doreen interrupted. "I know, I know, I know.
We'll drive up to Phoenix and treat your Aunt Rainy to a steak dinner at a nice restaurant. Ooh, or I-talian, or seafood. Wouldn't that be nice? We owe her so much."

"We do," Purdy agreed. Doreen's sister's name was Loraine. Among Doreen's family the sister's names rhymed – Dough Rain and Low Rain – but the sisters were Dodo and Rainy to each other. Loraine had taken them in when they lost their house, after Purdy's father disappeared. She took care of Purdy when his mom gave up searching and could do little more than lay in bed for months.

"Well done," said Joe, as soon as Purdy was alone.

"You saw all that?" said Purdy.

"It was beautiful. I knew you'd find a clever way to give her the money, but that was art. Much better than anything I could have thought up. And the way you faked not knowing. If you weren't so smart you could be an actor."

"Yeah," said Purdy, "you'll make me into a good liar yet."

"Well, I don't see any harm in a little lie now and then if it's to help someone."

"Hmmm. I'm not so sure."

"So, what was it you wanted to talk about?" said Joe, changing the subject.

"Oh, nothing important. I've been thinking a lot about Sockworld lately." Now, Purdy knew, he was really lying. He had been doing much more than thinking about Sockworld. He did not know why he was hesitating about telling Joe he had become a resident of Sockworld himself. Something about the idea of meeting Joe in person scared him, though he could not imagine why.

"Really?" said Joe. "Have you figured out a way to get me out yet?"

"No. Sorry."

"Of course that's why I went to that physics conference. I can't help but think the answer has something to do with physics. You know, the movement of energy through space and time. I was hoping they'd talk about layers of reality. Closest they came was one speaker who was talking about alternate universes, and said every kind of universe you can think of is possible."

"That can't be right."

"Why not?"

"Because it doesn't make… it's not logical. If any universe is possible that would mean no universe is possible."

"You mean because 'no universe' would be on the list?"

"Yeah. Everything includes nothing. I know that no universe is not right, so everything being possible can't be right either."

"Huh. Well, I'm no scientist," said Joe. "Maybe I misunderstood. Like I said, it was all a bit over my head. Anyway, you said you've been thinking about Sockworld?"

"Oh, yeah. Just wondering about stuff like, um, do people die there?"

"I… I imagine they must. I mean I've never seen it, but no one lasts forever. People are so spread out here, if I didn't see someone for a long time I wouldn't know if they died or just moved someplace else, you know?"

"I get it. What about getting old, then?"

"Well, I can't look in a mirror, but the picture, the image of me I had when I got here seems to be the same. Except…"

"Except?" said Purdy

"Well, you'll think it's my imagination, but my hand, the one that punched the guy."

"Yeah?"

"It was only in your world for a second but it came back looking different. A little bruised, maybe a little older looking than my other hand."

"Does it hurt?"

"No, no, I don't feel a thing. It just looks a little different to me."

"Pee-culiar."

Joe laughed. "You sound like your mom."

"People always say that when I answer the phone. I hope my voice changes soon."

"I don't. I like your voice. Anyway, don't worry. It will come down in time. Time brings everything down."

17

A light rain was falling, and it rained most of the day, which was un-usual. Rain in that part of the world, when it came at all, was usually heavy but brief. Purdy awoke with a fever. His mother took the day off work so she could hover over him. She had always been a hoverer when he was sick. She came into his room from time to time to push the moist hair from his forehead and check his temperature, bringing him more medicine and cool compresses when the fever ran high. For the most part, Purdy was unaware of her, falling in and out of sleep most of the day, having strange dreams. When he did awaken, the darkness of the day confused him and he was unsure whether it was day or night. The bor-ders between sleep and wakefulness blurred, the dreams lingering when his eyes were open. Sometimes he dreamed of Sockworld and then, upon awakening, would clutch at his sheets to make sure he was not still floating.

After studying weather in the third grade he had acquired the habit of looking up whenever he stepped outside to see what the sky was up to. The clouds that day would have interested him. By evening both the clouds and his illness had passed.

The next day Purdy finally had his opportunity to launch his carefully planned interrogation of Savitri. He smiled when he entered the classroom and saw Creighton's vacant desk. Savitri's desk was also vacant, but she came in a minute after he did.

"What happened to you yesterday?" she said.

"I was out sick."

Savitri leaned back in her chair. "It's not catchy, is it?"

"Nah. You should be fine as long as you don't kiss me."

"I'll try to control myself."

"So," said Purdy, "did I miss anything?"

"No, not much."

"People still talking about Creighton? Trashing a classroom for no rea-son – that was weird, huh?" He watched her response carefully.

"Yeah, weird. I couldn't talk to him on the weekend. He's totally grounded."

"Oh, yeah, you guys are neighbors." Purdy was pleased to find that his own involvement in the incident didn't seem to be common knowledge. Now he would toss the secret information he had into the fire to see what sparks flew up. "I heard some guys talking about you two last week."

Savitri leaned forward. "What did they say?" she asked eagerly.

"Oh, nothing much."

"What did they say?" she demanded.

"It's dumb. They were thinking you were Creighton's girlfriend. Stupid, right?"

"What else did they say?"

"Aren't you upset that they would say bad things like that about you?" asked Purdy.

Savitri seemed confused by the question for a moment. "Huh? Oh, yeah, sure. Boo hoo. OK, I'm over it. Now tell me what they said or I'm going to punch you."

"Well, let me try to remember," said Purdy. "It was last week…"

"Purdy," she said threateningly.

"And I've been sick." He fake coughed.

"Purdy, you better."

"OK, OK. They were talking about a rumor."

"Ooh, a rumor," said Savitri. "What about?"

"About you helping Creighton with his homework."

Savitri's smile disappeared. "Oh. Is that all?"

"You mean it's true?"

"Yeah, so what?"

"I don't get it," said Purdy. "Is he forcing you to somehow?"

"What? No. It was my idea."

"I'm confused," said Purdy.

Savitri beckoned for him to lean forward. She began whispering. "It's all part of my evil plot. I'm new at this school and I want to be popular. What's the fastest way to get popular?"

"I don't know."

"No, you wouldn't," said Savitri. "You hang around with the popular kids. Creighton is the most popular boy, so I told him I'd do some of his homework for him. That way people would see us hanging around together. It's working. Yesterday I started sitting at the popular table at lunch. My evil plot is working." She sat back, a glowing neon portrait of satisfaction.

Purdy had to take some time to absorb the strange story. While he didn't understand why being popular was important, he could see how the method Savitri outlined might work. There was, however, something missing, something she wasn't saying. Then it struck him. "Oh my gosh," he said. "You like him. You like Creighton."

"He's OK," Savitri said, averting her eyes.

"But don't you know what a big jerk he is?"

"Of course."

"Then I don't get it."

"OK, Einstein," said Savitri, "I'll explain it. Yes, Creighton is a jerk, but what you don't get is that all guys are jerks. You might as well try to get a good-looking one."

The conversation that Purdy thought would clear up all his questions had left him more confused than ever. Although they had a friendly relationship in school, Purdy did not consider Savitri a friend. According to his strict classification of such matters she was a classmate, a school acquaintance. To be a friend he would have to see or talk to her outside of school, but he did not, except for accidental meetings at the Stop 'N' Shop. Now the finding that she liked, and likely loved Creighton placed her squarely in the enemy camp. Although true adherence to his classification of her would not allow for it he experienced a sharp sense of loss.

He began to feel dizzy. Afraid he would disappear in the middle of the classroom he took a bag of M&M'S from his pocket and popped a few into his mouth.

"Can I have some?" said Savitri.

"No," he replied sternly, then handed the package back without looking at her. After a few hundred years the lunch bell finally rang. As Purdy made his way toward the cafeteria he was suddenly flanked by Creighton's friends, Rod and Javier.

"We have a present for you," said Rod.

"From Creighton," said Javier.

"He's just so thoughtful that way," said Purdy. "If it's chocolates I hope he knows I don't like nuts. That's one reason I don't like him, actually."

They escorted him up to a row of lockers and stopped. "Is the present in a locker?" Purdy asked.

"No," said Rod, "you in a locker – that's the present."

Purdy turned to look around and see if anyone would help him. The crowd already starting to gather had the party attitude of crowds that, in earlier years, had gathered around guillotines and gallows. "OK, OK," said Purdy. "Don't push. I know the drill." He bent his head down and squeezed into the locker that had been opened for him. "Just don't…"

The locker door slammed.

"…slam the door," said Purdy. He heard the lock click. "Open up," he yelled, and banged on the door, but he did it just for show. In a few seconds he appeared in the kitchen of his home. He searched the refrigerator door and found the piece of paper that had the phone number of the school office. He dialed the number on his cell phone.

"Hello," he said, "This is Purdy Hooper. Can you hear me? I'm in a locker. A locker. Two boys, Rod and Javier, stuck me in a locker. Locker 823. Yes. OK, thank you."

In a few moments Purdy was back inside the locker. Through the slots in the door he could see the crowd part. Rod and Javier came forward, with Principal Hughes holding each of them by the shoulder. There was the sound of the lock opening. Purdy stepped out with his cell phone in one hand and a half-eaten fried chicken leg in the other.

18

On the scale of exciting pets, hermit crabs rank a few steps be-low lizard, and only a step or two above pet rock. Being nocturnal, they rarely emerge from their shells when you can see them. When they do emerge they are genuinely alien looking, with an assortment of strange legs and claws, and a pair of tiny, unblinking eyes at the end of thin stems. Not a pet that easily elicits affection. Purdy was genuinely fond of his crab, however, because it was interesting, and because it was his. He liked all animals, dogs most of all. He had often longed to have a dog when he was younger, but he knew there are no happy endings to dog stories, and he did not think his mom was up to any more loss.

When he got home from school he ate some ice cream. Still feeling a little depressed he decided to clean his room. He often cleaned when he was depressed. He began with the hermit crab tank. There were several shells in the tank. He picked up the one that contained his crab, the other shells being the crab's spare clothes. He peered inside and said hello. He popped the crab into his shirt pocket and began scooping the sand with a sieve to remove the tiny dots of crab poop. His phone rang and he realized he had forgotten to make the "I'm home safe" call to his mother.

"Hi, Mom. Sorry, I forgot."

"No problemo senor," said Doreen. "Listen, darlin', today was the store's anniversary or some such and the boss brought in Chinese food from Tucson. Well, there was way too much so he gave me a bunch to bring home. Isn't that exciting? We'll have real Chinese food for supper."

"Nice, but will you want to eat it again?"

"Oh, I only ate a few bites. I didn't want to eat it at work. You know how Chinese food gives me such bad gas."

"Yes," said Purdy. "Well, there's something to look forward to."

"Oops, got to go. See you later darlin'."

Purdy put the lid back on the crab tank. The urge to clean had had a mercifully brief life. He decided to fly around town for a while. He disappeared into Sockworld but had not flown far from his home when he got the feeling he was being watched. He looked down and noticed a pair of eyes peeping out of his shirt pocket. "Oh, my gosh, Claw Machine, I forgot to put you back." He flew back to his room, appeared, and returned the crab to its tank, where it quickly scuttled over to its favorite corner and retreated into its shell again. "Sorry about that," said Purdy. "Now that I know you can travel with me I'll take you to the beach, once I learn how to find my way back."

Once back in the air he began to wander aimlessly around town. This haphazardness was not his general way of operating. Purdy was a planner, a researcher, a maker of lists. Sockworld brought out a different side of him, however, and each flight was a willing leap into the unknown.

While moving quickly down the main street of town something odd registered upon his peripheral vision and he swung around to take a second look. Through the barber shop window he saw a man floating above the heads of the barber and his customer. It was a young man, reclining on his side, watching the television set that was up on a high shelf in the corner of the shop. Could this be Joe at last, Purdy wondered. He approached the man slowly.

"Howdy," said Purdy.

"Uh huh," replied the young man, not taking his eyes off the TV.

"I'm Purdy."

"Can you wait for a commercial?" said the young man irritably. Purdy was relieved to hear it was not Joe's voice and waited for a commercial.

"Howdy," he repeated. "My name's Purdy."

"OK," said the young man.

"What's your name?"

"My name is Richard. My father's name was Richard. And his father's name was Richard."

"That's nice. And your great-grandfather's name?"

"Lloyd." Richard scowled and turned back to the television.

"Wait," said Purdy. "I bet people called him Richard. I bet that's why he named your grandpa Richard."

"Oh, yeah, maybe. I never thought of that. I bet that's right."

"Sure it is," said Purdy. "So you like watching TV?"

"Yeah, don't you?"

"Of course," said Purdy.

"Do you have a remote?"

"A remote?"

"A remote." Richard stuck his hand out and waved his thumb up and down, the universal sign of a remote control. "I'd give anything for a remote."

"No. Sorry. Wish I did."

"Yeah, me too."

"There are lots of TV's in town. Why do you watch in the barber shop?" asked Purdy. "Do you know someone here?"

"Nah," said Richard. "I used to like barber shops. When I was a kid my mom didn't let me read comic books, but there was a table full of comics at the barber shop. Also the mirrors."

"The mirrors?"

"There were mirrors in front and behind, so when I sat in the chair I could see hundreds of Richards, thousands of Richards."

"Richards all the way back."

"Yes!" Richard smiled, but the smile left him when he looked in the mirror. "No more Richards now."

Purdy looked and saw that the barber and his customer were reflected in the mirror, while he and Richard were not. The commercials ended and Richard's full attention returned to the television. Purdy waited for the next commercial so he could say goodbye. "Well, I guess I'll be going now," he said.

"Uh huh."

"Nice to meet you."

"Uh huh. Be careful."

"Careful?" said Purdy. "Why? Of what?"

"Someone's coming to take us away. The bird lady said so."

"Oh, her." Purdy recalled his encounter with Madame Bruneau. "I wouldn't worry about it. I don't think she knows what she's talking about."

"She does talk funny. Maybe you're right."

As Purdy left he turned once more to look through the window of the barber shop. He wondered what Richard did when the barber turned off the TV. Perhaps he wandered the town each evening like a moth looking for a flickering TV light.

<>

Later that evening the cardboard containers of Chinese food were pushed toward the center of the kitchen table, and Purdy and his mother sat back in their chairs, too full to move. "That was G-triple O-D good," said Doreen. "I wonder if anyone has ever exploded from eating too much?"

"Depends on what kind of explosion you're talking about," said Purdy.

"I don't want to hear that kind of talk. You're going to ruin dessert."

"Dessert?" Purdy groaned.

Doreen pushed herself up and retrieved two fortune cookies from the kitchen counter. She held them out. "Which do you want?"

"Fortune cookies are…"

"No," Doreen interrupted. "We agreed. Don't you dare. You already ruined horoscopes for me."

"I simply pointed out that there are approximately seven billion people on the planet. If you divide that by twelve zodiac signs it means that you share your sign with over 583 million people, and 583 million people can't all be having a good day for business with romance on the horizon."

"OK, you win. So, so, so that's why fortune cookies are more scientific. One fortune, one person. See, you ain't the only one who can do math."

Purdy laughed and held out his hand. "I'll take the one on the left."

"I'll go first," said Doreen. "It says, 'You have a pleasant unexpected surprise in store.' See, that could happen."

"OK, first of all, all surprises are unexpected."

"Just hush and read yours."

Purdy broke his cookie and pulled out the fortune. He read it to himself and scowled. "See, this is so general. I hate general fortunes. I want a fortune to tell me I'm going to get hit by a bus on Tuesday at 2 o'clock."

"What does it say?"

"It says, 'If you can't take it, leave it. If you can't leave it, take it.' See? That doesn't mean anything. That doesn't… oh my gosh."

"What's the matter?"

"Oh, nothing," he said, but in his head he kept repeating, "I've got to find Joe."

19

How do you find someone who isn't there? After days of hoping to avoid meeting Joe in Sockworld, now Purdy knew he had to meet him, but did not know how to find him. Joe had no address, no phone, no e-mail. Purdy didn't even know what he looked like, or what his real name was, so couldn't describe him should he come across some other occupant of Sockworld. He took out a blank piece of paper and drew a rough map of Casi Nada with a black marker. With a red pen he drew a large grid over the town. He first considered searching the town square by square. He realized, however, that he was searching for a moving target, and there was nothing stopping Joe from entering a square that had already been searched. Next he located the center of the town and marked it with an X. If he began at that point and moved outward in a spiral he might have less chance of missing Joe. Again he discovered a flaw in the plan. The spiral search was not three-dimensional. Joe might be in any part of any building, he might be above the clouds, or beneath the ground. Clearly any sort of search would be hit or miss, with miss being far more likely.

At last Purdy saw that he had gone about the problem all wrong. He went to his closet and pushed away piles of books until he located a box of old toys, in which he found what he was searching for – a box of thick sidewalk chalk. He got up extra early the next morning and walked out to the end of the street that led up to his trailer park. He began to write with light blue chalk on the black street. To an old woman walking by with her beagle it appeared he was just making long random lines. From high above he knew that Joe would easily be able to read the words "meet me." If he could not find Joe he would have Joe find him.

As he sat in class later that morning he thought about what he would say to Joe when he met him. Savitri tapped him on the shoulder. "Hey, are you sleeping?" she said. "I said where are all the cows?"

"What? What cows?"

"I've been living here a while now, and I've seen plenty of cowboys but no cows. How can you be a cowboy without cows?"

"I doubt you've seen plenty of cowboys," said Purdy. "Not everyone in a cowboy hat is a cowboy."

"I think I know a cowboy when I see one. They come in their pickups Friday nights to load up on beer and whiskey." Savitri crossed her arms and smiled. "Go on, admit I've seen cowboys."

"All I'll admit is you may have seen a few cowboys, and a bunch of alcoholics dressed as cowboys. There are no cattle ranches near here that I know of. Southern Arizona is pretty dry, so it takes a lot of acres to graze one cow. There are some ranches east of here, down near the border, but if you like cows you'd have a better chance of seeing them up north."

"What's that supposed to mean?" said Savitri angrily. " 'If you like cows'?"

"It doesn't mean anything."

"You think because my family's from India I like cows?"

"What?"

"You think I have a live cow wandering around my living-room at home?"

"What? Whoa, ding, back to your corner," said Purdy. "You're having this fight all by yourself. I didn't say anything." He took a small package of tissues out of his backpack and handed it to Savitri.

"Thanks." She wiped her eyes. "Sorry, I told you I'm a little sensitive… about certain things."

"A little," Purdy laughed. "Look, I don't know how it was in New Jersey, but no one here cares if your family's from India or Indiana. Look where we are. The Indians, um, Native Americans have always been here. The Mexicans have always been here. Heck, this was part of Mexico before we stole it. If anyone should feel out of place it should be me. I'm like the whitest kid in town."
Savitri laughed. "Don't make me laugh," she said. "You'll make me forget I'm mad at you."

"Mad? What for now?" This reminded Purdy that he had made up his mind not to speak to her anymore.

"Creighton says it's your fault he got in trouble," said Savitri.

"He's talking now, huh? What did he say?"

"He said he was chasing you but you kept disappearing."

"Oh, I see," said Purdy. "So it's my fault because I didn't stick around and let your psycho boyfriend beat me up?"

"Yes. No. I don't know. He's not a psycho. What did he ever do to you?"

Purdy paused. He would have liked to tell her, but he was still saving that information for blackmail purposes. "I refuse to talk without my attorney."

"Whatever." She handed him back his package of tissues and said quietly, "Thanks. You were right. It was pretty bad in New Jersey."

"Sorry."

"Yeah," she said, and wiped her eyes again. "I don't know why we always have to fight."

"I don't mind."

"Seriously? You like fighting?"

"No," said Purdy. "I don't like to fight, but at least it's not boring."

"Oh, so now I'm boring?"

"Oh, jeez. Let's change the subject. So, I hear there are lots of cows in New Jersey."

"Purdy, I'm going to kill you."

Purdy spent the whole day at school expecting to be found by Joe, and then the whole evening, and the whole weekend. He theorized that Joe either didn't see the chalk, or perhaps was out of town again. Joe's voice did not greet him when he got home after school on Monday. He parked his bicycle in the back yard where he found his mother relaxing on a lounge chair. It was one of her days off work. She had sunglasses on so Purdy was not sure if she was awake until he noticed the beer can in her hand.

"Hey, Mom," he said.

"Hello, darlin'. How was school?"

"Boring as usual."

"That's nice. Do you want me to make you a snack?"

"Nope. Relax. I've been making my own snacks since I was six."

"My little man," said Doreen. "I'll be in soon."

"OK."

"Purdy?"

"Yep?"

"Don't ever drink. It ain't ladylike."

"OK."

After a peanut butter and salami sandwich, Purdy decided to go outside and watch for Joe. He entered Sockworld and flew up through the roof, hovering over his trailer. After a while he heard the sound of distant thunder, which surprised him as there was not a cloud in the sky. As he wondered about how far sound could travel he was hit with another sound, thunderous but not thunder, and right in back of him. He turned and came face to face with a huge African lion. The lion shook its tangled mane and yawned, revealing an arsenal of large yellow teeth.

"N-nice lion," Purdy said. The lion seemed to be backing up but Purdy noticed, too late, that it was crouching down, preparing to spring. All he could do was duck as the massive cat flew over him. To his relief it did not turn and attack, but simply kept floating away, looking back over its shoulder as if to gauge the success of its prank.

In the distance Purdy saw a man float past the lion, patting its flank as he passed. As the man drew closer something about his thin face and brown hair seemed familiar.

"Joe?" Purdy called. The man drew up before him. Purdy's face was puzzled. He whispered, "Dad?"

<>

20

"Purdy, you're here," said Joe, who turned out to be Ronald Hooper, Purdy's father. "I wish I could be happy to see you, but this is bad, this is very bad."

"Why?" said Purdy, wondering if more lions were on the way. Joe seemed to shake, and he turned from side to side, grasping at his unfeeling hair. "I had hoped so hard you'd never get stuck here like me," he said. "Your mother won't survive this."

"But…"

"No, I know her. When I disappeared it was very hard on her, but having you to take care of made her hang on. With you gone…"

"But listen…"

"She won't survive," shouted Joe, "and all we can do is watch."

"But I'm not stuck!"

"What?"

"I'm not stuck," said Purdy. "I can pop in and out of Sockworld whenever I want. That night after I almost got kidnapped I figured out how to do it. Turns out those dizzy spells of mine are like a door."

Joe looked him up and down. "Show me."

Purdy looked around to make sure no one could see him, then he crouched down and appeared atop the roof of the mobile home. He rapped the roof with his knuckles to prove he was out in the real world, then disappeared into Sockworld again. "See?"

"That's amazing," said Joe, then he seemed to deflate. He started to say "Purdy" but his voice caught, and he put his fists over his eyes as he shook with sobbing. "I'm sorry," he said at last. "I'm happy to see you. I really am."

"So I see. Me too," said Purdy. "But why didn't you tell me who you were?"

"I thought it would freak you out."

"Duh, yeah," said Purdy, "but I'd be over it by now!"

"Didn't you ever wonder why I hung around you and your mom? Did you ever think it might be me?"

Purdy considered. "I did dream it was you once, but I never dared think it." The father and son stood gazing at each other.

"I'm surprised you recognized me," said Joe. "You were so young when I disappeared."

"I've seen pictures."

"Oh, yes. Of course."

"Shouldn't we hug or something?" said Purdy.

"Well, you know we won't really feel anything, but sure, why not?" They clitched together for a moment then moved apart.

"Yeah, nothing," said Purdy. They both laughed. "So, Joe, I mean Dad…"

"You can still call me Joe if you want. You're used to it. Your mom used to call me Joe. She never liked Ronald."

"OK," said Purdy, "so, why the heck didn't you tell me you've got lions here?"

"Oh, only one," Joe said, looking back in the direction the lion had gone. "The old king is harmless."

"That's the old king?"

"Yes, poor old thing. I imagine he must have been a circus or zoo lion at one time. He's bored, well everyone here is, so he tries to amuse himself by pouncing. Did he scare you?"

"Oh, no," said Purdy. "I get attacked by lions so often it doesn't bother me anymore. Yes, he scared me!"

"Sorry I never mentioned it then, but I thought you'd find it hard to believe. Anyway, I never imagined you'd be here," said Joe. "This is going to be so nice. Now you can visit, and see me when I talk to you."

"It is nice to see you and know you're not… you know."

"Dead?"

"Yeah. You're not, right?"

"No," said Joe. "So what's going on? What did you send for me for? I saw the writing on the street."

"Oh, yeah. I've got something important to show you. Wow, this is going to be better than I thought. Meet me in my room in a minute." Purdy dove down through the roof.

When Joe arrived Purdy asked him to put out his hand, and then placed something in it. Joe opened his hand. "A shell?" he said.

"Wait."

After a few moments the shell stirred and claws and beady eyes emerged. "Oh," said Joe. "Your crab. Is that what you wanted to show me? Of course I've seen it before. I'm not sure I understand. Are you giving me your pet to keep me company?"

"No!" Purdy took the crab, popped into the real world to put it back in its cage, then popped into Sockworld again. "Don't you see what I did?"

"I see you're very fast going in and out of Sockworld. I wish I could do that."

"Joe, I'm sorry but sometimes you're so dumb. Are you sure we're related?"

"Pretty sure."

"If I can take my crab in and out of Sockworld I can take you. I'm going to take you home."

Joe's expression flickered back and forth from astonishment to doubt. "Would that work?"

"I don't see why not."

"When?"

"Now," said Purdy, "unless you've got some packing to do."

"No, no, all I've got is what I'm wearing, and a few extra socks."

"Look, if you're going to cry again I've got to tell you it's getting a little annoying."

"I'll try not to but I can't make any promises," said Joe. "I'm not as strong as I once was. What do I do?"

"Take my hand," said Purdy. They joined hands. "Adios Sockworld." In an instant they were standing on the ground.

"Whoa," said Joe.

"I know," said Purdy. "The gravity really hits you if you're not used to it." He looked up at Joe, and then circled around him. "Your hair – it just got a little grey."

"Did it?" He looked around but there were no mirrors in Purdy's room. He took a stapler from the desk and gazed at his reflection in its shiny silver side. "Well, the picture of me in Sockworld was an old one. I suppose time has just caught up with me. Years… I've been watching all along, you know. I was there at your kindergarten graduation. At all your school events. Still, I feel I've missed so much, so much. Do you suppose we could re-do that hug?" Without waiting for a response he threw his arms around Purdy, lifted him off the ground, and spun him around.

The scent of his father's shirt seemed somehow familiar. Purdy had a sudden vision of his father spinning him around in the front yard of their old house in Phoenix. Purdy could not have been more than three at the time. He did not think he had any memories that went that far back.

"I felt that hug," said Joe.

"Me too," said Purdy, still wondering about that ancient memory. Just then he heard his mother's voice.

"Knock, knock, who are you talking to?" said Doreen, as he pushed open the door of his room. At the sight of her missing husband she collapsed in a heap on the ground and covered her face with her hands. Purdy and Joe looked at each other.

"It's OK baby, I'm back," said Joe, putting a hand gently on her shoulder.

Doreen fiercely batted his hand away. "Don't you 'baby' me," she shouted. "All these years not knowing if you were alive or dead, not a phone call, and you think you can just show up?" She roughly wiped the tears from her face with her arm. "Where have you been? Why couldn't you call? At least that?"

"I couldn't," said Joe.

"Why not?" said Doreen. "Were you in prison? Even prisoners get a phone call."

"It's true, Momma, he couldn't" said Purdy. "He was in Sockworld."

"Where?"

"It's hard to explain," said Joe. "We've been calling it Sockworld. It's another dimension of this world that you can't see, hear, or feel."

"It's true," said Purdy. "I've been there too. You can fly around and go through walls and stuff."

Doreen gave them the sort of look she might have given aliens emerging from a U.F.O. "What is wrong with you?" she said. "You're trying to tell me all these years I've been in hell and you've been in Wonderland?" She struggled to her feet and lurched form the room. Her bedroom door slammed.

"We could have planned that better," said Joe.

"Ya think?" said Purdy.

<>

21

"**W**on't you please let me talk to you?" Joe said outside Doreen's closed bedroom door.

"Go away!" she shouted

Joe turned to Purdy. "I don't think there's any way to explain this that she'll believe," he said, "unless…"

"Unless she sees for herself?" said Purdy.

"Would you mind?"

"No. No trouble."

"Thank you, son. I'll wait in your room."

Purdy knocked on the door. "Mom, I'm coming in." He disappeared and reappeared beside his mother's bed. Doreen was draped sideways across the bed with her face buried in the blanket. "Mom?" he said.

Doreen leapt up. "Purdy, how did you get in here?"

He disappeared again. "Up here, Mom," Purdy said from atop her dresser, then disappeared again.

"Purdy?" Doreen stood up.

Purdy appeared behind her by the closet.

"How? What?"

"It's real, Mom. Sockworld. The only way you'll understand is if I show you."

"Show me what?"

"Take my hand." He took her hand a moment then released it. "We're here. In Sockworld."

"We're in my bedroom."

"Look down," said Purdy.

When Doreen looked down she saw that her feet were not touching the ground. She bent to see what she was standing on and tumbled over and over in the air. "What's happening?" she screamed. "Please, God, I'll never drink again."

Purdy latched onto her arm and she righted herself. "Takes a little practice," he said. "Come with me." Doreen screamed again as they shot through the roof and flew high above the town.

"Stop screaming," Purdy said. "You won't fall, and you can't get hurt here. I'm pretty sure." As they flew he did his best to give her a crash course in Sockworld. His talking was interrupted at times by screams, but they grew less frequent. He flew her in through the front door of the supermarket. They stopped before an old woman who was talking to a bagger.

"Can you tell me where I can find jello in boxes?" said the old woman.

"Aisle seven," said Doreen, out of habit.

"She can't see or hear us," said Purdy.

"Gee, I'm not sure," said the bagger. "Let me ask."

"Aisle seven with baking supplies," said Doreen.

"Can't hear you," said Purdy. "Go ahead, try and touch her." Doreen shrieked when her hand passed through the old woman's arm.

"This is the world Dad's been stuck in all these years," said Purdy. "Don't know how he slipped into Sockworld in the first place, but once in he couldn't get out. He's not like me. I just learned to pop in and out. No one else here can."

"He followed us from Phoenix?" asked Doreen.

"Yeah, must have. You can fly really fast here. Faster than cars. He's been near all along."

"My poor darling'." She took Purdy's hand again. "I don't like this place."

"The supermarket?" said Purdy.

"Not the supermarket, Sockworld. Take me home please."
In moments they were back in Purdy's room, hovering in front of Joe. "My poor darlin'," Doreen said to him.

"He can't hear you yet," said Purdy.

"Purdy, everything OK?" asked Joe.

"Yeah," Purdy said, answering them both. In an instant he and his mother were back on solid ground.

"My poor darlin'," said Doreen, and flung her arms around Joe's neck. "I didn't know."

"Little tomato, everything's OK now," said Joe. Both of them were crying, but soon the tears gave way to kisses. Purdy turned away smiling. In the midst of this ocean of familial bliss a small wave of sadness crossed over him, the thought that no one would ever love him as much as those two people loved each other. It was a strange thing to think, and he shrugged it off.

"You'll have to excuse me a minute," said Joe, extricating himself from his wife's embrace.

"Where are you going?" Doreen said, and clung to him so hard that one of his sleeves came off his shirt. "I'm sorry."

"It's OK," said Joe laughing. "It's an old shirt."

Doreen stood staring at the sleeve. "These are the clothes I described to the police when you disappeared."

"Yes," said Joe. "I'm sorry, but I haven't peed in nine years." He left the room.

"Wait for it," said Purdy.

"For what?"

There was a loud bang. "Ouch," said Joe.

"Got to open doors now," called Purdy.

Doreen ordered pizza for their celebration dinner. She started telling Joe all the things that had happened during his absence. The second time Joe said, "But I know," Purdy kicked him under the table and shook his head no. He knew how much it meant to his mom to tell her stories, and supposed it would relieve her of some of the burden she had been carrying to talk it all out. So they sat for hours at the kitchen table, listening to Doreen's stories about Purdy's first day of school, and how she taught him to ride a bicycle, and about her various jobs, and about living with her sister. Purdy excused himself to go to sleep.

"Good night Darlin'," said Doreen. "Turn off your alarm. I'll call the school. No school tomorrow. It's a holiday."

"Purdy," said Joe, "thank you. I know you're a big guy now, much too big for a good night kiss from your old man, but I've missed you so much. Do you suppose I might just give you a kiss on the top of the head?"

"A little weird, but yeah." Purdy lowered his head. "Knock yourself out."

"Wait," said Doreen. "Where's my camera?"

Soon Purdy's head was on his pillow. He looked at the light under his door and listened. For the first time since he was a small child he fell asleep listening to the muffled sound of his parent's laughter.

<>

22

In the morning, after a late pancake breakfast, Joe called a family meeting. "That's so exciting," said Doreen. "A family meeting. Purdy, why didn't we ever have one of those?"

"We did. We just called it something else. We called it talking."

Joe and Doreen took a seat on the couch and Purdy sat down in the beanbag chair he used for watching television. He scanned his father's face, looking for some echoes of his own features, but found none. He wholly resembled his mother, so far as he could tell. Would his nose grow large like his father's? Would his eyelids droop? He found Joe's face, now in 3-D instead of the flat old photos he had been studying for years, fascinating.

"Purdy, we need to discuss your ability," said Joe.

"You make it sound like I only have one."

"OK, I'll be more specific. Not your ability to be sarcastic or argumentative. I was referring to your ability to pop in and out of Sockworld. I know you've only recently acquired it. Have you had a chance to think about what you might do with it?"

Purdy had been thinking about it, and had even begun making list of things he might do in his journal. "Yeah, lots of things," he said. "Besides travelling, I could help people. Like if a building was on fire I could find where people were trapped without getting burned."

"And how would you get this information to the firefighters? 'Excuse me, Mr. Fireman. I can turn invisible and fly and there are still some people in room 517.' How could you tell them in a way they would believe?"

"I… I don't know. I'd figure it out."

"Well, it's admirable, thinking of using your ability to save people," said Joe. "Most boys your age would be thinking of peeking in the girl's locker room."

"I didn't say I wouldn't do that too."

Joe laughed. "We'll make some rules about that later. Ouch!"

Doreen had punched her husband in the arm. "We'll make the rules right now," she said. "You ain't gonna do it, understand?"

"Yes, Momma."

Doreen punched Joe again. "You're supposed to be setting an example," she said.

Joe winked at Purdy. "I've been thinking about this too," he said. "I was thinking I could take Purdy to Vegas. We could make his college money in one weekend."

"No, ut-uh, no way," said Doreen. "First off, it's cheating. You ain't even allowed in Vegas."

"Whoa," said Purdy. "Stop the presses. I thought he used to be a math teacher. Is Joe some kind of criminal?"

Doreen looked at her husband before answering. "Criminal? No."

"I was never arrested," said Joe.

"He was never arrested," Doreen said cheerfully.

"Oh, Lord," said Purdy.

"It was a thing," said Joe, "a fad. Card counting. Building assumptions based on the cards out on the Blackjack table. Not cheating, though the casinos reached a different conclusion."

Purdy sat forward and rubbed his eyes with the palms of his hands. "Mom, I don't get how you two ever got together. You're so honest and he's so… not."

"Well, he told me he was honest when I met him," said Doreen. "He lied."

"I did," said Joe. "Really, Purdy, don't get the wrong idea. I'm as honest as the next guy. I only lie for good reasons." He nudged Doreen. "Anyway, we're getting off the subject. I was hoping you might use your ability for science. For example, you could observe animal behavior up close. No hiding in a bush with binoculars. You'd be right out on the plains of Africa among a pack of hyenas, or high in the tree canopy of the Amazon jungle, following a spider monkey through its day. You could swim with dolphins and whales."

"It ain't natural," said Doreen, "invading the privacy of some poor monkey. The whole thing ain't natural. I wish he'd give up Sockworld altogether."

"I don't think he could," said Joe.

"Why not?" said Doreen.

"Yeah, why not?" said Purdy.

"Purdy, do you remember that story you wrote about Crab Boy and the robbery? Did you ever think how similar that was to the real thing that happened later at Mr. Kaapoor's place?"

"No, I never… it's just a coincidence," said Purdy.

"Is it?" said Joe. "See, I think your connection to Sockworld had been growing for some time before you actually went there. Eventually it was so strong you were able to hear me. You think you made up that story, but I think you remembered it – from a dream. A Sockworld dream. I think you were connecting to Sockworld in your sleep before you ever went there awake."

Purdy thought about this and had to admit to himself that it seemed possible, even likely. Nevertheless, he did not relish the idea that things might be happening to him that he was not in control of.

"Do you like Sockworld?" asked Doreen.

"At first it was scary," said Purdy, "but once I knew I wouldn't get stuck… yeah, I do." He thought about how when he rose into the air the world seemed to tip up and present itself to him. "It's kind of cool."

His mother sighed, and said, "Well, then, maybe it's meant to be."

"Which brings us to the main purpose of this meeting," said Joe. "Have you told anyone, besides your Mom and me, about your ability?"

"No," said Purdy. "I thought I'd show Savitri first, and maybe eventually take my whole class on a fieldtrip."

Doreen and Joe looked at each other and then back at him.

"What?" said Purdy, made nervous by their stares.

"No one can ever know," said Joe.

"Yeah, right," said Purdy. His parent's gaze remained. "What, are you serious?"

"Very," said Doreen.

"Why?"

"Purdy, you're a good person," said Joe. "If everyone was like you or your mom there would be no problem. Think of it – if everyone could access Sockworld there would be no more need for cars or airplanes. Pollution would be cut in half. It would be wonderful. Trouble is, most people in the world are not like you. Most people are no damn good."

"Not most," said Doreen.

"What would you say, fifty percent?" said Joe.

"There's some good in everyone."

"I'm not talking about some good."

Doreen thought it over. "Maybe twenty-five percent."

"Thirty-five percent?"

"Thirty percent."

"Done," said Joe. "OK, so at least thirty percent of the people in the world are no damn good. Now you think of Sockworld as a way to fly around, and maybe help people if you saw they needed help. What would a bad person use Sockworld for? A way to go anywhere, steal anything, kill anyone. If a bad person knew about you they would try to use you, use what you do. No one would be safe."

"And bad people have bad secrets," said Doreen. "They wouldn't like thinking little invisible you might be watching them at any time. They'd feel a good sight more comfy if you were out of the way. You know, d-e-a-d."

"Son," said Joe, "for your own safety, for everyone's, no one can ever know."

"Oh, man," said Purdy. He got up and began to pace. He had never anticipated the dire scenario that had been drawn for him. "What if I wore a mask?"

"Yes," said Doreen, "and I could make you a cape, and I saw some precious boots in a catalogue."

"Oh, man!" He plopped back down in the beanbag chair, all his fantasies about impressing his schoolmates with his super powers evaporating.

"Listen," said Joe, "keeping this a secret is a good thing. If you were famous it would distract from your schoolwork."

"Maybe helping people was the reason you were given this gift." Said Doreen, "but helping people ain't always easy. People who need help don't always ask for it. People who ask for help don't always need it. You'll need a good education to know what from which."

"So you've got to promise – no popping into dangerous situations," Joe said, and waited for Purdy to nod. "If there's a kitten stuck in a tree then yes, go for it. Right now concentrate on school. I just want you to have as normal a childhood as possible."

"Yeah, good job so far," said Purdy. He knew the moment the words were out of his mouth that he had made a terrible mistake. Joe's head bowed down under the weight of the words.

"Purdy!" said Doreen.

"I'm sorry," said Purdy, getting up and kneeling in front of Joe. "I didn't mean it."

"It's OK," said Joe. "There's something you need to understand. My disappearing all those years ago and messing up everything for you and your mom – it was just something that happened. It was nobody's fault. Do you believe me?"

"Sure."

"I want you to say it," said Joe. "It's important. It was nobody's fault."

"It was nobody's fault," Purdy repeated.

Joe reached out and tousled Purdy's hair. "Good boy. What I said before – I meant there's time. Time to be a kid. You're special, and…"

Doreen began crying.

"What's the matter?" said Joe.

"I don't want him to be special," she sobbed. "I want him to be happy."

"Maybe I can be both," said Purdy.

"No you can't, no you can't," she wailed, and left the room.

"It's been an emotional couple of days," said Joe. "What do you say we go out and play catch?"

"Catch?" said Purdy.

"It's a father – son thing."

"I know what it is. I don't have a baseball."

"Football?" asked Joe.

"No."

"Hamster?"

"What? That's sick. No."

Joe tossed him the remote. "Catch," he said. "OK, now you throw it back."

The meeting was over.

<>

23

"Purdy, wake up," said Doreen. "It's just a dream."

Purdy sat up, his pajamas heavy with sweat. His mother and father were standing by his bedside. "What?" he said.

"You were having a bad dream, darlin'," said Doreen. "You were shouting, 'No, no, no!'"

"Do you want to tell us about it?" said Joe.

"Let me think. I was at school. My old school in Phoenix," said Purdy. "There was a kid with a gun."

"Someone you knew?" said Joe.

"No, I don't think so. He was in a classroom, then he got shot. That's all I remember."

"How awful," said Doreen. "Don't watch no more scary shows on TV for a while."

"Babe, could you get Purdy a glass of water?" said Joe.

"He won't drink no water," said Doreen.

"I don't like the taste," Purdy confirmed.

"Water has no taste," said Joe.

"I can taste it."

"How about some chocolate milk then?" Joe suggested.

"Sure," said Doreen, and left the room.

"It wasn't just a dream, was it?" said Purdy. "It's going to happen."

"Maybe so."

"What do we do?"

"Nothing we can do," said Joe. "If you knew the name of the kid, or the date it would be different, but you can't very well go to Phoenix and say you had a dream about some unknown kid bringing a gun to school at some unknown time. At best they'd think you're crazy. At worst, they'd arrest you."

"There must be some way."

"Look, bad things happen. They always have, they always will. You can't stop that."

"But if I know," said Purdy, "then it's my responsibility."

"It's not. It's only your misfortune to know. Not your responsibility."

"I don't agree. I should at least try to help. How can I not?"

"Easily. People do it every day. Every day we all know there are hurricanes, floods, famines, every sort of mess in the world, but we don't all rush off to Africa or Asia, or wherever, to help. We live our lives. You can't help everyone. You have to make a choice. All you owe to the world is to live as good a life as you're able. You'll have your own share of troubles to deal with. Don't go looking for more."

Doreen returned and handed a glass to Purdy. "Sorry it took so long," she said. "We only had a drop of chocolate syrup left so I had to melt a chocolate bar, but that made the milk warm so I had to put ice in."

"Mom, this is root-beer."

"Sorry, darlin', I couldn't help myself. It was really good chocolate milk."

Once his parents left the room Purdy debated going back to sleep, for he feared returning to the same bad dream. Sleep presented the more persuasive argument and Purdy awoke to his alarm. His short vacation was over. He would return to school, his mom to her job at the supermarket, and his dad would look for local work until he could resume his teaching career.

While parking his bicycle in front of school, Purdy felt a tap on the shoulder. He spun around.

"Hey, take it easy, cowboy," said Savitri. "Too much coffee."

"Sorry," said Purdy. "I thought it was… someone else."

"Yeah, Creighton's back. So, where were you yesterday? Sick again?"

"No, no, um, my dad's back. I think I told you once that he went away when I was little. Now he's back."

"Is that a good thing?"

"Oh, yeah," said Purdy. "A little weird, but good." He started walking toward the school entrance but Savitri grabbed his backpack and pulled him back.

"Weird how?" she said.

"Well, my mom's all in love of course. He's my dad so I feel like I'm supposed to love him too but, well, I practically just met him."

"Do you like him?"

"Oh, sure."

"O M G. You want my advice?" said Savitri. "Shut up. Liking is more important. Love is only what you have to do."

"I don't think that's the way it works."

"It is. OK, so I have a little brother and sister," said Savitri. "I love them and all, but they are unbelievably annoying. I don't really like them. Is that terrible?"

"A little," said Purdy.

"You're an only child – you don't know anything."

Savitri was always hard to win an argument with, but Purdy thought he saw a way how he might win this one. "OK, so what about the other kind of love, romantic love? You don't think that's something you have to do, do you?"

"Sure," said Savitri. "Take my parents. They had an arranged marriage – you know, their parents picked them out for each other."

"People still do that?"

"Maybe not as much, but yeah. So my parents had to love each other because they were married."

"I'm going to have to ask for a judge's ruling on this," said Purdy. He made a buzzer sound. "EEEEE! Sorry, arranged marriages do not count as romantic love. I'm talking about falling in love first."

"No one really does that. They confuse being in love for being hot for someone. So you're hot for someone, you hook up, and then when you're stuck with them you have to love them or break up. So, yeah, love is something you have to do."

"Darn," said Purdy. "Thought I'd win that one."

"Please, you know as much about love as a squirrel knows about trigonometry."

Purdy was mulling over various snappy comebacks when the first bell went off, relieving him of the problem. They hurried into the building. As they were walking toward their classroom Purdy saw, standing in an alcove between some lockers, the boy with the gun that he had seen in his dream. "Watch out, he has a gun," he shouted, and pulled Savitri behind him.

"Impressive," said Savitri. "You just saved me from a cardboard turtle. What a dork." She walked away.

The boy Purdy thought he saw had vanished, and standing in his place was a large cardboard cutout of the school's mascot, Speedy the desert tortoise. "What's going on with me?" he wondered. "All this Sockworld stuff is too much. It's too much. I've got to get back to real life." When he turned away from the tortoise he saw Savitri and Creighton standing in front of the classroom. They seemed to be arguing. Savitri then turned and walked back toward Purdy.

"Everything OK?" said Purdy.

"No, not really. Sorry." She took a large cup of water from behind her back and splashed it down the front of Purdy's pants. "He made me. He said he'd tell about the homework. My parents would kill me."

"It's OK," said Purdy. "Go. Go!"

Savitri turned and ran into the classroom, pushing past Creighton.

Purdy walked into class carrying his backpack in front of him. He slid into his chair, listening to the familiar taunt of "got to pee?" He had to concentrate very hard for a minute to keep from crying. "Real life sucks."

After school, he found no one home. He knew his mom would be at work, but thought Joe might be there. He had a quick snack, called his mom, then popped into Sockworld to see if he could find where Joe had gone. He took a few turns above the town without seeing him, then gave up and went to the highway to play. Jumping over cars on the highway was much more challenging than it was on the streets of town. It was like reaching a higher, more difficult level in a video game. No sooner had he jumped over one car than another was right there. Often he had to jump three or four cars at a time before there was an opening to land and jump again. The big trucks were even harder to master because he had to jump so high so fast.

While he was jumping over a bus he noticed a man floating by the side of the highway watching him. Because he was distracted he let several cars pass through him. The last to pass through him was a small do-it-yourself type moving truck. He was surprised to see that the cargo section of the truck was packed with people.

<>

24

The man floating by the side of the highway had disappeared. "Had he been there at all?" Purdy wondered. He decided to catch up to the moving truck and see what was going on. He zoomed ahead, catching up easily. The men in the cab of the truck both had mustaches and were smoking cigarettes and conversing loudly in Spanish. Purdy flew back into the cargo compartment. It was dark but for the light of a couple of flashlights. There were twenty men and women sitting or lying on the floor. Some of the women were crying. The men were quiet, and most were fanning themselves with their hats. A couple of men had their faces pressed to the floor by the back gate trying to get some fresh air. It was clear to Purdy that this was a group of illegal immigrants, and that the driver and his associate were coyotes, professional human smugglers. Now he wished he had not seen it, had not gone back to look. Having seen it he felt he had to do something, though what that something was he didn't know. He'd always had sympathy for migrants. He could never understand what all the fuss about them was about. They were poor people, like himself, and most had nothing more nefarious in mind than to try to make a better life for their families. The coyotes, on the other hand, had very bad reputations. He had seen stories on the local news of coyotes abandoning locked truckloads of immigrants, leaving them to die in the desert heat. Other stories showed police coming across housefuls of immigrants held prisoner while the coyotes tried to extort ransom from their families.

He tried to imagine what his parents would advise. Joe would probably say that it happens all the time so there would be no point in trying to stop this particular truck. As for his mom, she would want to make sure the migrants were not in danger. Purdy's mind was made up. He would have to stop the truck. He thought the migrants might be angry about that decision, for they would lose the money they had already paid the coyotes and would get deported, but at least he could be sure they were safe.

He flew off into the desert and appeared. His hands searched his pockets for his phone until he remembered that he had plugged it in to charge when he got home from school. He couldn't call the police, so quickly devised a new plan. He required a disguise. Luckily, he was wearing an undershirt beneath his shirt. He took off his shirt, then pulled his undershirt up over his head and tied it in the back, creating a ninja mask which left only his eyes visible through the neck-hole. He put his shirt back on. All the while a lizard stood doing pushups on a nearby rock. Purdy envied the lizard at that moment. There were no moral ambiguities in its life, no need to decide between two bad choices. The lizard woke up each day with only one item on its to-do list – "Be a lizard. Check."

His disguise complete, Purdy disappeared and once again caught up to the truck. His plan was to appear on the roof of the truck and wave at the other drivers, whom he assumed would call the police to report the crazy person atop a moving truck. He appeared near the front of the roof but made the mistake of appearing on his knees. The truck was travelling at 70 miles per hour, so Purdy was hit with a 70 mile per hour wind that knocked him on his back and sent him sliding toward the back of the truck. He managed to flip over and desperately clawed at the impervious metal to slow his approach to the precipice. He slowed, but not enough.

His legs went over the edge and left him clinging to the top of the truck by his hands and elbows. This served to attract the attention of the drivers behind the truck. They began honking, and swerving to change lanes. A car pulled beside the truck and a passenger rolled down her window and yelled and pointed. The coyote driver, not understanding what she was trying to communicate, sped up and began swerving in and out of traffic.

Though never athletic, Purdy was sufficiently motivated to pull himself up a bit. He swung one leg and then the other onto the roof. He could have disappeared at any time, but did not want to do so because it would be seen. He crawled forward, then got up on his knees again, better prepared this time, and waved at the other traffic as if he were on a float in a parade. After several minutes, he could hear a siren in the distance. When the siren got closer and louder the truck pulled off onto the side of the road. Purdy dropped off the side of the truck that was away from traffic, disappearing before he hit the ground.

The coyotes leapt from the truck and ran into the desert, leaving the back of the truck locked. Purdy flew into the cab of the truck to see if the keys were there, but he didn't find them. In the back of the truck the migrants, having heard the siren, were in turmoil. Some screamed and banged on the back door, while others shouted, "Silencio," and argued with those trying to get out. A highway patrol car pulled up behind the truck. Two more patrol cars would arrive before one of the officers took a pair of clippers out of his trunk and snapped the lock off the truck's back door.

From above, Purdy watched the migrants meekly file out. They stood in line to be patted down and have their hands zip-tied behind them. One man broke from the line and started running into the desert. A patrolman fired his gun into the air, and the man stopped instantly and walked back to the line. The bullet passed harmlessly through Purdy's chest.

The migrants sat down by the side of the highway as an officer walked down the line with a jug of water and gave each one a drink while they waited for the bus that would take them to an immigration detention center. A helicopter arrived and began searching the desert for the coyotes and the masked daredevil that drivers had reported seeing on top of the truck. Purdy rose higher. From the vantage of fifty feet in the air the scene below seemed very peaceful. He wondered how high he would have to go before it would look as if he had done the right thing.

Turning back toward town, he was surprised to see the man he had seen earlier, floating a short distance away. He removed his mask and approached slowly. The man was of middle age, and had small, sleepy, wide-set eyes, a sharp nose, and dark, greased-back hair. He wore a black suit.

"Those are some slick moves you got," said the man.

"Oh, thanks. I'm Purdy."

"The name's Bradley Brown, but most people call me Buster. Get it? Buster Brown. Anyhows, I guess you know that already." He spoke quickly, in some sort of New York accent.

"No," said Purdy. "How would I know your name?"

"Aren't you one of them?"

"One of who?"

"A Fed, a G-man."

"I'm a kid."

Buster turned his head and looked Purdy over out of the side of his eyes. "Oh, yeah. I thought so, but it could have been a disguise. So, what are you in for?"

"What do you mean?"

"What did they nab you for? Whaddya do?"

Purdy realized Buster literally thought Sockworld was a prison. "I didn't do anything."

"Oh, sure. I get you. I'm innocent too. That lousy J. Edgar Hoover had me pegged as a commie, but it wasn't true. This dame I was, uh, I was seeing dragged me to a couple of meetings but I could tell right off it was all a load of hooey. All that talk about everyone being equal, but all the commies ever delivered was an equal place in the bread line."

"You must have been here a long time," Purdy ventured.

"I've lost count, but my enemies I don't lose count of, and Hoover's on top of my list."

"You have a list of enemies?"

"List of people I'm going to kill when I get out of here. I got a few scores to settle, but Hoover, yeah, Hoover is Buster's enemy number one."

Purdy was chilled by the dispassionate way Buster discussed his hit list.

"I think you can cross him off. I'm pretty sure J. Edgar Hoover is dead."

"Is that what they're saying now?" Buster laughed. "Don't you believe it. He's an octopus, that guy. He's got his hands in the pockets of the newspapers, the radio stations, you name it. You can't believe anything you hear."

"That's true," said Purdy. He had decided that Buster was not his ideal cell-mate, so he started slowly backing away from him. "Well, nice to meet you. I've got to be going."

"Hey, not so fast. I need your help," said Buster.

"Help?"

"Yeah. I'm busting out of here, and you're going to help."

<>

25

"Sorry, I really can't help you,"** said Purdy, still trying to back away.

"Listen, kid, I've been tailing you for a while now," said Buster. "I've seen the way you slip in and out of here, easy-peasy. I've seen you talking with some other guy, and now he's out."

"I don't know what you're talking about," Purdy lied, realizing that Buster must have seen him talking to Joe before he took Joe out of Sockworld.

"So that's the way you're going to play it. OK, have it your way. I didn't see nothin'."

"Well, it was nice to meet you, but I've got to go."

"Sure, sure, see you around," said Buster.

Purdy turned and began speeding toward town but when he looked back to see if he was being followed he found Buster was clinging to his right ankle. "Dude, seriously?"

"What?" said Buster.

"Let go. You're embarrassing yourself."

"No I'm not."

"You're acting childish."

"Am not."

"Oh, for Pete's sake!" Purdy reached down and tried to pry the man's hand off his ankle, but in Sockworld everyone was evenly matched in being essentially powerless. It was like one shadow trying to push another. "Let go!"

"I'm sticking to you like a three cent stamp until you take me out of here."

"I'm not," Purdy insisted.

"Are too."

"Oh, jeez." Purdy thought that if he could not pry off his parasitic hitchhiker perhaps he could scare him off. He dove down straight into the highway traffic, at first weaving between the oncoming vehicles, then hitting them head on and passing through them. All the while Buster screamed like a child on a roller coaster, but continued to hold on tight.

Purdy flew into town, looked around, then headed for the glass factory. He flew down the top of the short smoke stack into the center of the white hot furnace. Blinded by the bright flames he could not tell if Buster was still with him. He emerged into the relative darkness of the factory.

"What a ride," said Buster, still clinging to his ankle. "Again, again."

"Shut up."

When he flew outside he was surprised to see Joe standing at the factory entrance shaking hands with another man. He didn't pause to see what that was about. He needed to get rid of Buster first, but was running out of ideas. "If the situation was reversed," he wondered, "what would scare me?"

He rose high into the air, then turned and dove very fast toward the sidewalk. Instead of stopping he plunged into the ground, into darkness. He was instantly and completely lost. He did not know which direction was up. No matter which direction he turned he was still entombed in blackness. "Stop," he commanded himself to try to control his rising panic. "Think." Then he remembered Joe's advice on the subject. He relaxed and after several long moments his head bobbed up into the light.

He was surprised to see Buster floating above ground waiting for him, apparently having refrained from tagging along beneath the surface. Buster lunged, but Purdy slid back under ground. He moved what he estimated to be five yards to the right and popped his head above ground, but Buster was watching for him and lunged again. Twice more he moved and popped his head up but each time Buster attempted to grab onto him. "I'm getting tired of playing the mole in this human whack-a-mole game," Purdy decided. "I'm just going to have to make a run for it." He burst into the light and flew as fast as he could into the sky. He was so high he passed through a cloud, and when he emerged Buster was once again clinging to his ankle.

"Oh, man!" said Purdy. "Will you stop that?"

"Sure," said Buster, "soon as you take me out of here."

"I told you, I'm not going to."

"Why not?"

"Because you want to kill people."

"So?" said Buster. "What's wrong with that? Haven't you ever wanted to kill someone?"

"Not until today," said Purdy. He decided he needed help so he dove down to search for Joe. He found him walking, a half a block from the trailer park. "Joe."

"Purdy, everything OK?" said Joe.

"Not exactly. There's this guy bothering me. He's grabbed hold of me and says he won't let go 'till I take him out of here. I guess he saw me popping in and out."

"Is he hurting you?"

"No, you know he can't. He's got hold of my ankle. I've tried everything but I just can't shake him."

"So take him out," said Joe.

"Yeah, like he said," said Buster.

"Shut up," said Purdy. "No, not you Joe. I can't take him out. He wants to kill people. He wants to kill J. Edgar Hoover."

"Not much chance of that," said Joe. "Listen, meet me in the backyard." Joe started running. When he arrived he said, "Purdy, I don't like the idea of anyone bothering you. Take him out. I don't think he'll be a danger to anyone."

"Are you sure?" said Purdy.

"Sure."

Purdy convinced Buster to hold onto his arm instead of his ankle so he would be in a better landing position. They both appeared. Buster fell to his knees, unused to gravity. "I'm free," he shouted, shaking his fists in the air. "Hey, what the…" His hands had become thin and gnarled, his hair went white. He was rapidly getting older. Then, all at once, he disintegrated into a cloud of dust, which a passing breeze carried into the neighbor's yard.

Purdy and Joe stood looking at the ground, at the metal cigarette lighter and belt buckle that were all that was left of Buster. "What just happened?" said Purdy.

"I think he was very old, maybe older than he should have been," said Joe. "Time caught up with him."

"Holy jeez. Wait, did you know this was going to happen?"

Joe hesitated. "I didn't know for sure. I thought he would get older."

"Why didn't you say something? We could have warned him."

"You were in trouble. I…"

"I was fine," said Purdy. "We killed him."

"Old age killed him."

"But, no, if he stayed in Sockworld he would still be alive."

"Being in Sockworld is not the same as being alive," said Joe. "You don't know. You're only a visitor. You can come and go. You're not stuck. You don't realize how much has been taken from those people. They can't feel, they can't smell, they can't taste. There's no real human contact. Almost all the pleasures of being alive are missing. Yes, you can see your family, all the people you love, but from the outside, your face pressed up to the candy store window but too poor to go in. Believe me, he's better off."

"Maybe," said Purdy, "but that was not your decision to make."

"My son was in trouble. I did what I had to do."

"It was not your decision."

<>

26

"Knock, knock."

"Come in, Mom." Purdy was lying on his bed staring at the ceiling. "You know, you don't have to say 'knock, knock.' If you actually knock it makes the same sound."

"But you wouldn't know it's me," said Doreen.

"I'd know."

"OK, then." She sat on the edge of the bed. "Your dad told me what happened. It must have been awful."

"It was. I never saw someone die before."

"I have, some few times. You know, that ain't the way it usually happens – poof – no. It was an unnatural way to die, but it was an unnatural way to live too. Poor man. Don't go beating yourself up about it. It wasn't your fault."

"But Joe…"

"No, not your Dad's fault neither. I'd have told you to do the same. Nature made a mistake and set itself right, that's all. Nobody belongs in there, you know."

"I know."

"If it were me, I'd take them all out."

Purdy sat up. "Are you kidding? They'd die."

"Some would, I expect, but maybe some ain't so old, like your daddy. Maybe they'd have a chance to go back to their families."

"I just couldn't take the risk of killing more people."

"Letting them go ain't the same as killing them."

"Call it what you want," said Purdy. "Dead is dead."

"Is it?"

Purdy was puzzled. "Oh, you mean heaven? You know I'm not like you. I'm not sure like you. I try to keep an open mind. I know billions of people have believed in it, and lots don't, but I don't know how anyone can be sure either way without evidence."

"Well, I don't know what to tell you darlin'," said Doreen. "Just keep that open mind – you never know what may fall into it. And keep thinking about those poor stuck people."

"I will."

"And what about the critters?"

"What about them?" said Purdy.

"Don't you think it's right to put a suffering animal out of its misery?"

"Yeah, I guess."

"And the animals in Sockworld are suffering, ain't they? I'll answer for them. Yes. Set them free."

"OK," said Purdy, "if I can catch them."

Doreen patted him on the shoulder, got up and left the room, and then came right back. "Knock, um, I mean…" She knocked. "I forgot to ask. Your Dad wanted me to find out how long you'd be mad at him."

"Another half hour should do it."

"Okey doke."

<>

At dinner, Joe announced that he had gotten a job at the glass factory. "During my years in Sockworld I'd flown through the glass factory many times," he said. "One day I saw the accountant working late. I looked over his shoulder and noticed something odd about his calculations. What was odd was that nothing was odd. All the incoming money had even amounts of change. When he billed customers he always rounded up to an even number of cents. When the money came in he applied only the uneven amount to their account. So on every transaction at least one cent, sometimes as many as nine, went missing."

"Who cares about a few pennies?" said Doreen.

"Nobody. That's exactly what he was counting on. The customers didn't care, and the factory got all the money it was supposed to. Over the course of a year, though, it added up to two or three thousand dollars missing from the books, maybe more. Money he paid himself, probably by setting up a bank account under the name of some fake supply company. It was really very pretty work, but I pointed it out to the boss and now I'm the accountant."

"And you're going to round the dollars up to even numbers?" said Purdy.

"Right." They all laughed. "So, babe," said Joe, "you can quit your job now."

"What? I ain't quitting," said Doreen. "I like my job. 'Sides, with two of us working maybe we can put money away for a real house, and for Purdy's college."

"I can pay for college myself," said Purdy.

"Don't be silly," said Doreen. "That's our job."

"But I can. Speaking of that, do you think I could have a metal detector for Christmas?"

"I don't know. Put it on your list. But you can't pay for college looking for lost change."

"Not change, meteorites," said Purdy. "I saw a documentary about a meteorite hunter who used an ultra-light airplane to search for meteorites on dry lake beds. Meteorites are sometimes worth thousands. Well, I don't need an ultra-light – I am one."

Joe leaned over to Doreen and said in a stage whisper, "If he asks for a spacesuit, don't get it for him or the next thing you know he'll be collecting moon rocks."

<>

The next day in class Savitri tapped Purdy on the shoulder. "Let's talk about it," she said.

"Let's not," said Purdy.

"I said I was sorry."

"And I accepted your apology. Move along citizens. Nothing more to see here."

"Why won't you discuss it?" said Savitri.

"Because."

"Because why?"

"Because it's a girl thing," said Purdy.

"What is?"

"Discussing. If one guy stabs another in the back they don't feel the need to sit down afterwards and talk about it."

"I see," said Savitri. "So you think I stabbed you in the back?"

"Not discussing."

"I told you, Creighton made me do it."

"Not discussing."

"I'm not doing his homework anymore," said Savitri. "Does that make you happy?"

"N.D."

"You are so annoying," said Savitri.

"Sorry you feel that way," said Purdy. "Want to discuss it?"

"Shut up."

Purdy turned away, but after a minute decided he might have been a little too mean. "Listen," he said, "all you need to know is that I'm not mad at you."

"Uh huh. So we're good?"

"I guess."

"See?" said Savitri. "It didn't kill you to talk like a girl."

Purdy sighed, then something occurred to him. "You said you're not helping Satan with his homework anymore?"

"Creighton. Right," said Savitri.

"Did you tell him yet?"

"Yeah, this morning."

"Did you make him think it was his idea?" Purdy asked.

"No, why would I?"

"Oh, this is not good," said Purdy. "How did he take it?"

Savitri shrugged. "Fine, I guess. Why?"

"This is not good," Purdy repeated. "You don't understand bully mentality the way I do."

"And you're some sort of expert, I suppose?"

"I'm a Ph.D."

"OK, doctor," said Savitri, "so what's the big problem?"

"Bullies can dish it out, but they can't take it. A bully hits you, everything's fine. You hit him, there's a problem. They have to have the power. You took the homework away. Maybe he didn't want you doing his homework, maybe he even hated it, but you took it away. You did something to him, so now he has to get you back."

"Stop," said Savitri. "This is so stupid. I mean, he's not even a bully."

"What?" Purdy said, his voice rising half an octave.

"You just don't get his sense of humor."

27

When he arrived at school Friday morning, a little earlier than usual, Purdy was greeted by Savitri's face. Not her real face, but a photocopy of a photo of her which was taped to the front door of the school. Beneath her face was scrawled the word "cheater." He looked around, then tore down the picture, crumbled it, and stuffed it in his pocket. When he entered the school he saw more than a dozen copies posted all around. He ran to collect them. He even pulled a few out of the hands of curious students. He thought that if he was fast enough he could gather them all before Savitri saw them. The trail ended at the boy's bathroom.

He cautiously pushed open the bathroom door. Creighton was taping a page above each urinal. Purdy bolted in, grabbed the pile of copies from beneath Creighton's arm and tried to tear them in half. He struggled, but the pile was too thick. Before Creighton could grab them back Purdy tossed them into a urinal and flushed it. Creighton shouted, "I'll kill you," and punched him, knocking him to the ground.

Purdy lay on the floor, the taste of blood in his mouth. He slowly propped himself up on his
elbows. "Why kill me?" he said. "Because you can? Is this what Darwin promised for the world? Survival of the meanest? Bully kids, bully adults, bully neighbors, bully bosses, bully corporations, bully governments? Kill me then, but make it quick because there are a lot of others who are smaller and weaker that you have to kill too. You have girls to kill, babies and puppies to stomp on, butterflies to punch."

Creighton had listened to this tirade patiently, and with evident amusement. When it was over he said, "Who's Darren?"

"Darwin, you monkey!" Purdy got to his feet, breathing hard, his heart pounding in his ears. "Well, go ahead, if you're going to kill me. I'm done running."

Creighton took a moment, then said, "Cool," and started toward him. Purdy said, "Oh, jeez," turned, and ran out the door. He ran down the hallway, looking through the windows on the classroom doors, searching for an empty classroom. He found one at last, entered it, and ran into the supply closet to disappear. Creighton was only steps behind.

"I saw you go in there," said Creighton. "You can't get away this time." Purdy heard a loud noise behind him. Creighton counted down, "Ten, nine, eight…" When he got to one he threw open the door, then stepped back slowly. A lion, the old king, stepped out of the closet. He shook himself, sniffed the air, and pawed at the ground, perhaps surprised to feel something solid beneath his feet. Then his gold eyes fixed on Creighton.

The lion sprang. Creighton shrieked, falling to the ground. The old king vanished in a shower of dust above him.

Purdy brushed the dust from his hands. He had been holding the lion's tail in case he had to make it disappear again. He was sorry to see the old king go. He looked down at Creighton, who was still on the floor, wide-eyed and whimpering.

"Bet you wish you had that diaper now," Purdy said. He stepped over Creighton and walked to the classroom door. He turned back and said, "This is the end. Tell all your bully friends. Bullying at this school is over. And if you're ever mean to Savitri again, well, I'll leave it to your imagination."

Creighton did not show up in class that morning. Purdy relaxed in his chair, and felt something in his back pocket. He took out a wad of paper and unfolded it. It was the first picture of Savitri that he had found on the school door. Savitri was seated behind him now and was, as far as he could tell, unaware of the events that took place that morning, so he quickly hid the paper in his notebook. He smoothed the picture with the palm of his hand and gazed at it surreptitiously. In the photo Savitri was standing in a kitchen, looking directly at the camera with a big accordion smile. It was a nice face, Purdy decided. How had Creighton gotten hold of a photo of her? She must have given it to him. Purdy closed the notebook.

<>

That weekend, Purdy and his parents travelled north to Phoenix to visit his aunt Loraine. Doreen prepared her sister for the reappearance of Joe by telling her that he had just gotten out of a prison in Mexico, where he had been held all the years he was missing, which her sister readily believed. Too readily, according to Joe, who had concocted the story.

Purdy tried to convince his parents to let him take them to Phoenix through Sockworld, and replace a long, boring, four to five hour car trip with a minute or two of flying, but Joe and Doreen had both resolved never to enter Sockworld again. "Besides," said Joe, "how would we explain how we got to Phoenix without a car?"

Loraine ran out of her house when she heard their car doors slam. She was a few inches taller than her sister, and her hair that week was blonde with streaks of blue. The reunion began, as it always did, with the two sisters hugging each other and crying. Then Loraine turned to Purdy. "Oh my goodness, will you look at you? How big you've gotten. Dodo, what kind of fertilizer do you use to grow boys this big?"

"Just love and junk food," said Doreen.

Loraine then approached Joe with folded arms. "So, Mr. Hooper, I see you're back. I've often thought 'bout what I'd do if I ever saw you again. Most of them plans involved beating you with a stick."

"I missed you too," said Joe.

Loraine smiled, threw open her arms, and gave him a hug. Then, while Joe and Purdy gathered the luggage, the sisters joined arms and chatted. Purdy always noticed that their accents got stronger when they were together.

"You got any men in there, Rainy?" said Doreen.

"I don't think so. You might just check under the bed, though. Good Lord, I can't keep track. Last week at the mall I nearly kissed a man who had just come up to me to ask if I had the time."

"What?"

"Well, he looked familiar, so for a moment I thought we were dating."

<>

The money Doreen had earmarked for this trip had been spent getting Joe new clothes, but Joe had gotten a small monetary reward for revealing the thief at the glass factory, and an advance on his salary, so they were still able to treat Loraine to a couple of restaurant meals during their stay. That night, at a favorite Italian restaurant, the sisters anguished over the menu.

"Everything looks so good," said Doreen.

"I know," said Loraine. "I could just lick the menu."

"Don't do that," said Purdy. "There would be germs."

"A few germs never killed no one," said Loraine.

"Uh, yes they have," Purdy said.

"Well, they probably had it coming."

"Purdy, how will I ever decide?" asked Doreen.

"Mom, you know you'll eat off everyone else's plate anyway. Why don't you just decide what you want us to eat, and we'll decide what you're having."

"Perfect!"

The waitress approached and said, "Are we ready to order?"

"You bet," said Doreen. "My sister will have the chicken cacciatore, my son will have spaghetti and meatballs, my husband will have the eggplant Parmesan."

"And for you?" said the waitress.

"She'll have lasagna," said Purdy, "and better bring some extra plates."

After the food had arrived Loraine pushed aside the Chianti bottle candle and leaned toward Joe. "Tell us about prison."

"It's not really suitable dinner conversation," said Joe.

"Oh, go on, Darlin'," said Doreen.

"Well, conditions were pretty harsh," Joe improvised. "I had to sleep on the floor with a rock for a pillow. There were cockroaches the size of housecats. The food was surprisingly good, though. The local women made these amazing tamales. I still dream about them."

"The women or the tamales?" said Doreen.

"Never mind that," said Loraine. "Did they beat you?"

"No. Sorry to disappoint you," said Joe. "No, they just locked us up and forgot about us. That's the thing that eats you from inside – the fear of being forgotten."

Purdy could tell Joe was no longer speaking of an imaginary Mexican prison. "Dad, try the garlic bread," he said. "It's really good. You'll stink for days but it will be worth it."

Joe laughed and was drawn away from the dark cell of memory.

28

During the car trip back to Casi Nada, Purdy stretched out in the back seat and marveled at how different his world had suddenly become. He had a father now, his mother seemed happier, finances would no longer be quite so precarious, and his bully problem at school was, ostensibly, over. Perhaps now life would at last become dull, that most underrated of states. Not boring, which was an active assault upon his mind, but dull, without the constant barrage of unpleasant surprises. That it would also be without pleasant surprises was of no consequence to him as he had long ago stopped hoping for those. This was evidenced by the last Santa letter he wrote, at age eight.

"Dear Santa,

How are you? I've been awful worried about global warming. I hope it doesn't melt the North Pole. You don't have to bring me nothing this year. Last year I asked for real x-ray glasses, a jet pack, and a set of Oxford English Dictionaries (the ones with the magnifying glass). You brought me a truck. It was an OK truck, but it wasn't on the list. I know lots of people like surprises, but I don't. They are most always ever bad, and if they're good they're not as good as you hoped for. Anyway, it's nothing personal. Say hi to Mrs. Claus and the reindeer.

Love,

Purdy

P.S. Please bring my mom something. She likes surprises."

<>

Monday was a half day of school because there was teacher training scheduled for the afternoon. At noon, Purdy rode his bicycle over to the Stop 'N' Shop to buy candy.

"Howdy," Purdy called as he entered the store.

"Terrible, terrible," replied Amar from behind the counter. "Come look at this."

Purdy came to the counter and looked at the small TV set Amar was watching. On the screen was a helicopter view of his old school in Phoenix.

"Such a shame," said Amar, "guns in schools."

Purdy felt his stomach drop. "When did this happen?" he asked.

"Now. It's happening now."

Purdy watched police cars speeding toward the school. "Sorry, I've got to go," he said.

"What's the matter?"

"I've got to…" Although his legs felt wobbly he made his way out of the store.

"Have some fruit," Amar called.

He passed his bicycle, ran around the side of the store and disappeared.

He flew to the highway. He held his arms out the way small children do when pretending to be an airplane. He did this, not for aerodynamic reasons, as there was no air, but to help stay aligned with the ground to prevent spinning. He urged himself to fly faster and faster. The cars blurred beneath him.

In less than a minute he was over the valley that contained Phoenix. Once in Phoenix he thought he would have a hard time finding his old school. He had planned, during his short trip, to triangulate with the mountain peaks he could see from his former schoolyard – Camelback Mountain to the east and Piestewa Peak to the North. The plan became moot as soon as he spotted the swarm of news helicopters.

He flew in low, past the police cars and fire engines, and the gathering crowd of frantic parents. He took a quick turn around the outside of the school but saw the windows were blocked off from the inside. He remembered the lock-down drills he had practiced when he had gone to school there. First there was a "It's sunset at school" message on the intercom. The classroom door was locked and the lights turned out. The windows were blocked off with black paper, and then the children and teacher would sit down on the floor in a tight, silent group. Someone from the office would come down the hallways trying each doorknob to make sure it was locked. It was that sound, the rattling doorknob, that used to scare Purdy.

He entered the school. Swat-team police with their masked robot faces were moving cautiously down the hallways. A group of students was being hustled out the front door. Purdy began flying through the classrooms. The first few were already empty. Then he passed classroom after classroom still in lock-down with students and teachers sitting in silence in the darkness, staring at the door. So far there was no shooter in sight, nor any sound of shots being fired. The whole school was eerily quie*t*. *"Is it over already?"* he wondered. *"Am I too late?"*

The school, like most of the elementary schools in Phoenix, was made up of single story buildings. The various wings of the school were arranged by grade. Purdy passed through the wing containing kindergarten and first grade classrooms. He moved on to the next wing, and it was there, in a third grade classroom, that he found the boy with the gun.

If he was a third grader he was short for his age, Purdy observed, and very thin, his shoulder blades poking through the back of his t-shirt like small wings. He had long, stringy blonde hair, and dark circles around his eyes. He paced slowly back and forth across the front of the classroom, the handgun in his right hand bouncing against his leg as he walked. The class sat on the floor in the back of the classroom, watching. No one appeared to have been injured. The teacher, a young woman, kept talking quietly to the boy. "Put down the gun and we can talk about this," she said. "It must be heavy. Put down the gun and we can help you." The boy with the gun did not pay any attention to her. He seemed to be waiting for something.

Purdy tried to figure out how to intervene without the class seeing him. *"If he puts the gun down on the desk maybe I could grab it and disappear so quickly no one would see me,"* he reasoned. *"He won't, though. If he starts to point it at someone I've got to disappear him, no matter what."* With this realization he began following closely as the boy paced back and forth.

"Put down the gun and rest. You must be tired," the teacher intoned. Just then the boy brushed the teacher's desk as he was passing and knocked a ruler to the ground. The students in the back of the class screamed at the sound.

"It's OK," said the boy. "It was just a ruler." He bent down behind the desk to pick it up and Purdy saw his chance. He crouched down and appeared beneath the desk, grabbed the boy's arm, and they both disappeared.

The boy pulled his arm away from Purdy and that action sent him spiraling toward the ceiling. Purdy flew up beside him and clitched onto his arm to steady him. He answered the boy's expression of fright and confusion by saying, "Yes, we're not part of that world anymore. Follow me."

Just then the police, alerted by the children's screams, knocked the door open. Purdy and the boy watched from above. The teacher pointed to her desk and the police rushed at it with their rifles, but they did not find the boy with the gun.

Purdy led the boy up through the ceiling and continued to a spot so high over the school that the sounds below were muffled.

"Are there any more of you?" Purdy asked.

"What?"

"Any more shooters? Any more kids with guns down there?"

"No." The boy gazed quietly at the school below. "I didn't feel anything," he said. "I was afraid it was gonna hurt, but I didn't feel it at all."

"Afraid what was going to hurt?"

"Dying," said the boy. "They must have shot me through the door or window. I never felt it."

Purdy realized he had a whole other situation to deal with now. "The kid has seen me, has seen Sockworld, and now he thinks he's dead. How can I return him now?" he thought. "I guess I could leave him here. Anyone who wants to shoot kids doesn't deserve to be down there. I could leave him up here. No, that doesn't seem right either. I don't know."

"You don't look like an angel," said the boy.

"Yeah, I get that a lot," said Purdy. "Do you mind putting that thing away?" He pointed to the gun. "It wouldn't work up here but it creeps me out."

"Sorry," said the boy, tucking the gun in his pants pocket. "Don't worry, it has no bullets."

"Wait, what? Did you already shoot them?"

"No. I never had any bullets."

<>

29

Trying to work through his confusion, Purdy returned to his dream. He had seen the boy with the gun, and he had seen him getting shot. Though he realized that he might have forgotten part of his dream, in the part he did remember he did not see the boy shooting. He felt annoyed at himself for calling the boy a shooter, for jumping to an understandable but wrong conclusion based on insufficient information. Why then, he wondered, did the boy do something so horribly wrong as bring a gun to school? To show off? To intimidate? The boy before him did not seem boastful or angry. He seemed oddly resigned to his own understandable but mistaken conclusion – that he was dead.

"I'm sorry," Purdy said, "I don't know your name."

"You don't? It's Simon."

"Simon, I don't get it. Help me understand. Why would you do something so stupid as bring a gun to school? You must have known that the police would come, that they might even shoot you."

Simon looked down, but said nothing.

"Oh my gosh," Purdy said quietly, "you did know."

The boy nodded. "I couldn't do it myself."

"But why? You're so young."

"I just couldn't take any more."

"Any more…?"

In response, Simon turned and pulled up his shirt. His back was covered with bruises, scars, and burns. He put his shirt down.

"Holy jeez, who did that to you?" Purdy asked.

"Don't you know? My mom's boyfriend."

"Didn't you tell her?"

"She knew, but she didn't do anything."

"Why didn't you tell the police?" Purdy said.

"Why would they care if my own mom…"

The two boys were reduced to silence. They floated a few feet apart and, to avoid each other's gaze, looked down and watched the scene below. Purdy did not know what to say to the boy or what to do with him.

"So this is heaven?" said Simon.

"Well, not exactly. Sort of an in-between place."

"I don't want to go to heaven."

"No one really wants to die," said Purdy.

"Oh, I wanted to die. I just don't want to go to heaven."

"Oh. Um, why not?"

Simon whispered, "Because I'm mad at him."

"At him? Oh, Him. Because he didn't help you either. I get that," said Purdy. "Lots of people get mad at Him sometimes. See, I don't think he's the kind of hands-on manager most people think. As long as the planets don't bump into each other too often he's pretty much happy." This gave him an idea. "Listen, I've got to go talk with my supervisors for a minute. I'll be just over there. Try not to move."

"OK," said Simon.

Purdy flew several yards away. He waved his hands intermittently to make it appear as if he was talking with someone. He thought about what he was going to say, and when his plan was complete he flew back.

"There's good news and bad news," said Purdy. "It seems you're not all the way dead."

"What?"

"Yeah, you're still sort of alive at this point, so my supervisors have decided to send you back."

"Back?" said Simon. "I don't want to go back."

"That was supposed to be the good news," said Purdy. "Listen, it won't be like before. Once the police find out what happened to you they won't send you back to the same situation. No matter what, that is over. Bad news is you screwed up big time bringing a gun to school, so you'll probably go to juvi for a while, but you didn't kill anyone, and you're only little, so it won't be forever. You have a second chance."

"Please, no. Don't send me down there again."

"Listen…"

"Please," said Simon.

"I know your family is pretty messed up. There's no excuse for them, but that doesn't mean everyone is bad. You have to find people you can trust…"

"Why can't you help me?"

"Well, I'd like to," said Purdy, "but you can't believe the red-tape you have to go through to get anything done up here. You can't rely on the angels up here to help you. You have to find the angels down there. There are some good people, people who would help you if they knew you needed help. You just have to find them and be brave enough to ask for help sometimes."

Simon turned away. Purdy gave him some time to think. Below, students continued to be led out of the school in greater numbers.

"Simon?"

"OK," the boy said quietly.

"What?"

"OK, if I have to."

"Good," said Purdy. "Just one thing before I take you back down there. Don't tell anyone that you saw me or went up to heaven, or anything like that. First off, they wouldn't believe you, and second…"

"They'll think I've lost it."

"Right." Purdy took Simon's arm. "If they ask where you disappeared to, just say you had to go to the restroom or something. Ready?" They flew down past the helicopters, over the crowds, and in through the open doors of the school. Police were still running up and down the corridors, searching. The boys arrived back in the same classroom they had started in, which was now empty.

"I'm going to have to leave you here now," said Purdy as they hovered. "I'm sorry about all the stuff that happened to you. Still, you were wrong to scare everyone so bad."

"I know. I'm sorry."

"I'm sorry too," said Purdy. "Sorry I called you a shooter."

"That's OK."

"I hope you'll have a better life now."

"I'll try. Thanks. Will I see you again?" asked Simon.

"No, not for a long, long time I hope."

"I don't know your name."

"Oh," said Purdy, "um, you can call me Joe. Good bye."

Purdy and Simon appeared and then Purdy released the boy's arm and immediately disappeared again, and rose up to the ceiling to watch. Simon looked down and drew the gun, suddenly heavy, from his pocket. A police officer appeared in the doorway. "Drop your weapon," he shouted.
Simon held the gun out and said, "It's empty."

The officer shot him.

"No!" Purdy screamed. "No, no, no!" He shot up through the ceiling and kept going, higher and higher. When he opened his eyes he was surprised to see the sky dark above him and the curved Earth below. He had reached the edge of space. Scared, he turned and plummeted back down. He landed in desert with no city in sight. He floated low above the ground. Wandering in the desert usually soothed him, but now he found its silence oppressive. It left too much room for his thoughts. Rising again, he scanned the horizon until he spotted the familiar mountains of Phoenix far in the distance. Soon he located the highway and sped home.

He overshot his home and landed on his knees in the backyard garden. The tears that he could not shed in Sockworld now blurred his vision. He stumbled to his feet and knocked down a plastic flamingo, which shattered. He stared at the pink shards of plastic at his feet. He uprooted another flamingo and smashed it to the ground, then went down the row smashing flamingos. He was screaming and did not hear his mother's voice at first.

"Purdy, what are you doing?" said Doreen. "Stop! Stop that!" She grabbed him around the waist from behind and swung him about. The memory of his father swinging him when he was a child flashed in Purdy's mind again. His rage subsided, and when his mother released her grip he sank to the ground.

"What good is it?" he said. "What good is what I do? I can't change anything. I can't help anyone."

"What are you talking about?"

"He begged me not to send him back, but I wouldn't listen."

"Who?"

"The boy with the gun. Now he's dead, and it's my fault."

<>

30

Doreen kneeled beside Purdy. "Just slow down and tell me what's going on," she said. "Are you talking about that boy on TV? I was just watching it. What does that have to do with you?"

"I was there."

"Purdy!"

"I went to stop him from shooting the kids. I had to. It turned out he wasn't there to shoot at all, he was there to get shot. I think they call it suicide by cop."

"But why?"

Purdy recounted his conversation with Simon. "…And then I said, 'good bye.' and left him, and he got shot anyway. It's all my fault. I killed him. If I had listened to him he'd still be alive."

"But he is alive," said Doreen.

"What?"

"They said so on TV."

"But I saw him get shot."

"Yeah, he got shot – in the shoulder," said Doreen. "He's in the hospital. He'll live. They also said on the news that his mom and her boyfriend were arrested, but they didn't say why. Now I know."

"He's alive?" Purdy said.

"Yes, Darlin'."

Purdy began to laugh. He was in that emotional state where laughter and tears are interchangeable. "He's alive!" His laughter soon stopped. He wiped his face with his sleeve. "Mom, I don't understand. What good is it all? What good am I? I knew what was going to happen but I couldn't stop it. What is the point of being able to do everything I can do if I can't help anyone?"

"You're right," said Doreen. "All that invisible flying crap can't help no one. Look at me." She lifted his chin. "It's you. It's you that helps. And you did."

"Oh, sure."

"You did. You gave that poor boy the idea that there could be a life past all his pain. Something to hang on for. Course you also gave him a pretty messed up picture of heaven."

Purdy laughed.

"Oh, my Lord," she continued. "I mean, I don't even know where to start. Your heaven was like an office run by a bunch of slackers. Well, maybe that's a good thing. Maybe he won't be in such an all-fired rush to get back there. You done real good. I'm proud of you." She stood up and brushed herself off. "When your dad gets home we can talk about your punishment."

"Punishment?"

"You promised not to pop into dangerous situations."

"But…"

"No one wants to hear your 'but'. You could have got yourself killed."

Purdy did not argue. "Mom, something else has been bothering me. Do you remember the last time you saw Dad, before he disappeared?"

"Yes, why?"

"What happened? Exactly?"

"Well, let's see. It was a nice afternoon in March. March is the nicest time of year, don't you think? Anyway, me and your daddy were having a fight about some dumb thing or other. I don't even remember what, ain't that funny? 'Cause so many times over the years I would blame his leaving on our fighting that day."

"OK," said Purdy, "so you were fighting?"

"Arguing. I shouldn't call if fighting. Don't want you to get the idea that we would hit each other. We never done that. Well, I'd punch him sometimes, but he never hit me. Your daddy is a gentleman. Not matter what, don't you never hit a girl."

"Promise. What I want to know is – when did you last see him?"

"Oh. After we'd fight… argue, your dad would usually go outside and let me cool down. So he went out in the yard."

"And where was I?"

"You? Huh, where were you?" Doreen closed her eyes to think. "You were out with your dad. You were so cute then. He was swinging you."

"What?"

"You loved to have your daddy swing you around. Last time I saw him was through the window. He was swinging you. Then I looked again and he was gone."

Purdy's worst fears were confirmed. His body contracted, bending him down until his forehead was resting on the dirt. "It's all my fault," he cried. "I left him in Sockworld."

"No you didn't," said Doreen. "You brought him back to the school."

"No, not the boy. Dad. He could never do what I do. The spinning must have made me dizzy. I took him to Sockworld and left him there. I ruined all our lives." He grabbed fistfuls of dirt with both hands and threw them on his head, as if trying to bury himself.

"Stop that," Doreen shouted.

"I made us all miserable. For years. It's all my fault."

"Stop." Doreen stepped away and let Purdy lie on the ground and sob for a while. Then she bent down and put her hand on his back. "Stop. Remember when your dad said it was nobody's fault? He made you promise that you believed it. I didn't know why then, but I do now. It's because he knew you'd figure this out someday, and he was right. It was nobody's fault."

"Yes it was. It was mine," said Purdy.

"You were just a baby. You couldn't control what you did. It was just an accident."

"No."

"OK, get up," Doreen said angrily. "You're only as good as your word. You gave your word to your daddy and you ain't gonna break it now."

Purdy pushed himself up. His eyes were red, and his face mud-stained. "I'm sorry," he said.

"Hush." His mom gave him a quick hug, then went inside. Purdy bent over and shook the dirt from his hair. He suspected that although his mom might believe that it had been just an accident, in her heart she would now blame him, if only just a little. He disappeared and floated through the house toward the bathroom, so as not to drop dirt on the floor. The TV was still on, still showing coverage of the shooting incident at the school. He paused to look at a class photo with Simon's face circled.

He found the bathroom door closed and heard his mother coughing and then throwing up. "Guess I really upset her," he thought. Soon he heard her slurping water from the faucet to rinse her mouth. Her eyes were red when she emerged from the bathroom. Purdy floated out of the way as she left so she would not pass through him. He waited until he heard the squeak of the couch springs before he appeared and closed the door to wash. When he was done he went to his room to take a nap.

Before too long there was a familiar knock. "Knock, knock," said Doreen. "Purdy?"

"What?"

"Someone's here to see you."

"I don't want to see anyone right now," said Purdy.

"It's Savitri."

"I don't…"

"Purdy, you get out here. She brought your bicycle."

<>

31

When Purdy entered the living room he found his mom and Savitri sitting on the couch looking through the family photo album, and eating potato chips.

"Purdy was such a gassy baby," said Doreen. "I swear sometimes when I was carrying him folks would think I was playing the bagpipes."

"Mom!" Purdy protested.

"Hey," said Savitri, "you used to be cute."

"Everyone used to be cute," said Purdy. "Thanks for bringing my bike back."

"No biggie. So, how dumb do you have to be to forget your bike at the store? Were you, like, pedaling down the street and suddenly realized there was no bike under you?"

"Something like that."

"You sure I can't get you something to drink?" said Doreen. "We got root-beer, orange soda, sweet tea."

"OK, a little tea, please," said Savitri.

From the kitchen Doreen called, "Purdy, why don't you ask your friend if she'd like to stay for supper."

"No thanks," said Savitri. "I've got to be getting home. I'm the oldest, and a girl, so my mom works me like a dog."

Doreen returned with the tea. "I'm the oldest and a girl too. High five."

Purdy realized he might have been the oldest too if he hadn't messed everything up. He'd often thought it might have been nice to have a brother or sister. He would have had someone to blame things on.

"Thanks," said Savitri when she had finished her drink. "I've got to go now."

"Thanks again for bringing my bike," said Purdy.

"You can't walk home," said Doreen, putting her hand on Savitri's shoulder.

"Sure I…"

"Purdy, your dad has the car. Take her home on your bicycle."

"What? I don't think that's even possible," said Purdy.

"Sure it is," his mother said. "My sister and I had to share a bike, so one of us would ride on the handlebars. Go ahead, you'll figure it out."

Purdy brought his bike up alongside the front steps and Savitri climbed onto the handlebars. Purdy pushed off, the bicycle wobbling badly.

"Can't you go straight?" said Savitri.

"I'm trying."

"Aaah, watch out for the mailboxes."

"How am I supposed to see with your big butt in the way?"

"You think my butt is big?" said Savitri.

"I didn't say that."

"Yes you did. You do, don't you? What are you doing looking at my butt anyway, perv."

"Oh, jeez."

"Aaah, watch out!"

They were riding on the sidewalk when a Chihuahua ran out in front of the bicycle. Purdy swerved and he and Savitri went flying onto a neighbor's lawn. They did not land hard or suffer any pain. Purdy's hand had slid down, found Savitri's wrist, and he disappeared both of them for just a second, setting them down gently. He knew it takes a while before a person realizes they are in Sockworld, and bet Savitri would not know.

"You OK?" said Purdy.

"I think so." She stood up and looked herself over. "Yeah, I am." She turned to the Chihuahua, which was running back and forth yapping at them. "Shut up!" she shouted. The dog ran off.

"I'm OK too."

"That was so weird," said Savitri. "You always hear how accidents happen in slow motion. It's true. It was like I floated off the bicycle."

"Well, we're not doing that again. I've got a better idea." He had Savitri sit on the bicycle seat, and he got in front of her and pedaled standing up, Savitri holding onto his waist. Soon they were in front of Savitri's small Pueblo-style house.

"Well, thanks for the near-death experience," said Savitri.

"Any time."

"Listen, will you come in for a minute. My mom's been wanting to meet you."

"Sure, I guess." He started toward the front door.

"Wait." Savitri blocked his way. "There's something I've got to tell you before we go in there. It's kind of funny, really."

"OK. So what is it?"

Savitri seemed to struggle with the words. "My mom…"

"Your mom?" Purdy urged her on.

"My mom thinks you're my boyfriend."

"What?" Purdy shouted.

"My mom thinks…"

"I heard what you said. Why in the world would she think that?"

Savitri took a couple of steps back. "I sort of told her."

"Oh my g… wait… you don't think… do you think I'm your…?"

"Please. O.M.G., no one is that desperate."

"Then why would you tell her?"

"It just came out," said Savitri. "She's always on my case about hanging around Creighton, so finally one day I just said, 'Stop worrying. He's not my boyfriend, Purdy is.'"

"Why me?"

"Because my parents like you. Don't ask me why. Maybe it's because you saved my dad's life, or something. Look, it's no big deal. It's not like you have to do anything."

Purdy thought it over. "OK, I guess. It's a little weird, but whatever." He started toward the door again.

"Wait," said Savitri, "there's one more thing."

"Oh jeez."

"You've got to promise not to hit me."

"Hit you?" said Purdy. "I'd never hit you. Wait, what is it first?"

"First promise."

"OK, promise."

"So, you being my fake boyfriend has been working out great," Savitri said. "My mom totally cooled her jets about Creighton. Anyway, my parents are always telling me about some nice Indian boy or other they want to fix me up with. You know, arrange a marriage. It's totally disgusting. It's like I'm some prize farm animal they want to find a mate for. One night, I just got so sick of it. I blurted out, 'Purdy wants to marry me.'"

"Holy jeez!" Purdy exclaimed. "You've got to be kidding."

"Look, they didn't jump at that one right away. I mean, you're far from perfect. You're not Indian. But, after a few minutes they sort of were OK with it."

"Well, that was nice of them. I can't believe this."

"It's no biggie."

"It is a biggie," said Purdy. "I'm twelve and I'm engaged."

"Not for reals. Stop being so selfish. My parents are off my case, and it doesn't cost you anything."

Put that way Purdy had to admit to himself that perhaps he had been over-reacting. "So, what's going to happen when I walk in there?"

"Nothing," said Savitri. "My mom's cool. She probably won't even mention it."

"You sure?"

"Sure."

"Is there anything else I need to know?" Purdy asked. "Do we have any kids?"

"No, but that's a good one. I'm going to save that one." She grabbed a fistful of his shirtfront. "Listen, you being my fake boyfriend is the best thing that ever happened to me. Don't screw it up."

32

Savitri led Purdy into her dimly lit living room. The first thing that struck him was how much neater it was than his own house. He felt as if he was looking at a display in a furniture showroom. There were a couple of couches, a large club chair, a few small tables and lamps, and a big screen television. The only indication that three children lived there was a naked plastic baby doll sitting on one of the couches. A small statue of Ganesha, the elephant-headed Hindu deity, sat on a shelf between a couple of spelling bee trophies.

"Mom, Purdy's here," Savitri called.

A small woman came bounding out of the kitchen, wiping her hands on an apron that covered a brightly colored dress. She crossed the room quickly, threw her arms around Purdy, and said, "Son in law!" Purdy gave Savitri a dirty look over Mrs. Kaapoor's shoulder.

"I am so pleased to meet you at last," Mrs. Kaapoor said. "Our family hero. Of course I have heard all about you."

"Nice to meet you," replied Purdy. It was then he noticed a small four-year-old girl peeping out from behind her mother.

"Ah, this is my youngest," said Mrs. Kaapoor. "Mimi, say hello."

Mimi eyed Purdy suspiciously and buried her face in her mother's dress.

"She's shy," said Mrs. Kaapoor. "Savi, where is Bob?"

"How should I know where the little prince is?" Savitri replied.

"Don't call him that."

"But it's true. He's the boy so he gets everything."

"We're not going to have this discussion in front of our guest."

Just then, a seven year old boy with dark, eager eyes emerged from the hallway.

"Bob, come meet Purdy," said Mrs. Kaapoor.

"Bob?" Purdy whispered.

"Hi," said Bob. "Do you collect Pokemon?"

"No," said Purdy. "I mean, I used to a long time ago."

"Do you want to see my deck? I have some really cool ultra rare cards." Without waiting for a response, Bob ran to his room.

"Come, sit." Mrs. Kaapoor put her hand on Purdy's back and shepherded him to the overstuffed chair, and sat beside him on the end of the couch, with Mimi beside her. Savitri stood behind the couch. "Why has it taken you so long to visit?"

Purdy sat transfixed by the small crimson dot on Mrs. Kaapoor's forehead. He had to keep himself from reaching out and touching it. Mrs. Kaapoor noticed his stare.

"Ah, that's called a bindi," she explained.

Purdy leaned forward and whispered, "Can you travel with it?"

"What a funny question. Yes, of course. I sometimes get some extra screening at the airport, but it's no problem."

Purdy sank back into the chair.

"So," said Mrs. Kaapoor, "I was so pleased to hear that you want to marry my Savitri. Of course, you'll have to ask her father, but that's no problem. He's very fond of you. Tell me, what was it that first drew you to my Savi?"

Purdy looked to Savitri for a hint, but she had turned away, shaking with laughter. "Her face, I guess."

"Yes, of course, she's beautiful," said Mrs. Kaapoor. "What else?"

Purdy groaned. "Um, her personality?"

Savitri had a coughing fit in an unsuccessful attempt to cover her laughter.

"What's so funny?" said her mother. "You do have a nice personality, when you want to. Here, take Mimi and go start the potatoes. I have some business to discuss with Purdy." As Mrs. Kaapoor handed Mimi over the couch, Purdy desperately signaled "no" and "help" to Savitri, but she just blew a kiss and left the room.

Mrs. Kaapoor sat back down and leaned forward. "Don't worry. I don't really think you're going to marry my daughter."

"You don't?"

"No, of course not. You're both so young. When I was your age I was in love with a different boy every week. I don't doubt that what you feel is real, but you may change your mind. Savitri definitely will, and that's OK. You'll have many lives, and many loves. Nothing lasts forever. Having a loving heart, that's what's important. Marriage – that wasn't your idea, was it?"

"Well, I…"

"I didn't think so. My Savi is so clever. Who do you suppose she gets that from?" She patted Purdy's knee. "Don't worry, we'll play along a while. Will you stay for dinner?"

"I'd like to, but I'm kind of in a little trouble at home, so I have to get back."

"You're a nice boy. I'm sure it's not too serious."

Bob ran into the room with his Pokemon cards, which Purdy dutifully admired. When he was done, Mrs. Kaapoor called, "Savitri, Purdy is leaving." Savitri walked him out. Once outside she asked, "What did she say to you?"

"Oh, she just wanted to make sure I was serious," said Purdy.

"And what did you say?"

"I said I love you more than pizza."

"Good, good, good," said Savitri. "My evil plot is working.

Purdy climbed onto his bicycle. "My family is planning to drive into

Tucson to see a movie this Sunday. Did you want to come along?"

"Sunday? Yeah, no. Sunday is Creighton's birthday."

"Oh, sure," said Purdy. "My invitation must have gotten lost in the mail. So, is he being OK to you?"

"I guess. Why?"

"I've just been wondering about him. Do you think his parents beat him?"

"Nah. I've met them," said Savitri. "They seem perfectly nice. He's just a jerk. Born that way, probably. Lately, though…"

"What happened lately?"

"That's the thing, I don't know. He won't talk about it, but something happened to him. He's changed. He's quieter, almost gentle sometimes. Lately he's the one following me around. You know, I never thought I had a shot with him, not really, but now I kind of think I do."

"You're welcome," said Purdy.

"What?"

"I said, 'you're welcome to him.' He's no prize."

"Yeah, maybe," said Savitri. "You want to hear the weirdest thing? He's afraid of you."

"Of me?" Purdy laughed.

"I know, right? Like anyone would be afraid of you, but he's always asking, 'Did Hooper say anything about me?' He's always saying, 'If he asks, say I'm nice to you.' It's totally weird."

"It is," Purdy agreed. "Anyway, wifey, I should get going."

"Yeah, me too, hubby dear."

"Just one more thing," said Purdy. "I want a divorce."

"Never," said Savitri. "You're stuck with me."

<>

33

When Purdy arrived home he found his father sitting on the front steps waiting for him. Joe patted the step beside him. "Come sit next to your old man," he said. "We'll talk. We don't get to talk anymore. I miss that."

"Yeah, me too," said Purdy, taking a seat.

"So, I hear you've been out killing people again."

"I thought I did."

"As your father I think I'm supposed to say something against that sort of thing. Well, it seems to me you made the best of an unfortunate situation. There's just something about guns. They always seem to attract the wrong kind of people."

"What kind is that?" said Purdy.

"People who like guns, for one, but beyond that, the angry, the weak minded. It's a crazy backwards country where children aren't safe in their schools but all we hear about are the rights of the shooters."

"That boy wasn't a shooter."

"Sure he was," said Joe. "Maybe he didn't have bullets but he caused a shooting. Think of the poor policeman who had to go home after shooting a child. It's all so sad. I take some of the blame."

"You?"

"I gave you bad advice," Joe said. "We knew this was coming, but I told you to forget it, that there was nothing we could do. You knew better, you did better. I'm proud of you."

"So no punishment?" asked Purdy.

"Now wait." Joe got up. "Let me think about that." He walked around and looked at Purdy through the bars of the handrail. "I'd love to punish you, I really would, but unfortunately, you're the kind of kid who punishes himself, which takes all the fun out of it for a parent."

"You heard about the rest?" Purdy said, looking down.

"I did."

"I left you in Sockworld. I ruined your life. All our lives. You must hate me."

"Do I look ruined to you?" said Joe. "I don't think I look that bad."

"You know what I mean."

"I do. Nothing is ruined. Accidents happen. We have to move on. As for hating you," Joe continued, "that's not even possible. When you were born your mom and I issued you a free pass."

"A what?"

"A free pass. It's a standard parental courtesy. It said, and I'm paraphrasing, 'You can irritate us, annoy us, disappoint us, anger us, even drive us crazy, but the one thing you can never do is make us hate you.' That's the free pass. Your teen years are coming up quick. Try not to use the free pass too often." He climbed the stairs, resting his hand on Purdy's head as he passed. "Are you hungry?"

"No," said Purdy.

"Good, more for me. Let's eat."

<>

Soon Purdy was sitting at the kitchen table with a plate of food before him.

"Do you like it?" Doreen asked.

When a new recipe was involved, this was always a dangerous question. If Purdy intimated that he didn't like a dish, his mother would say 'that's OK. Let me get you something else,' with the forced cheerfulness of a wounded soldier. A negative response hurt her in a way he didn't entirely understand. It was only food, after all. Saying he liked a dish was also problematic. Even if he did like it, saying he liked it might mean he'd get it over and over again until he hated it. Doreen was, undoubtedly, a frustrated cook, with too little time or talent to make the recipes she saw on TV come out right. She'd often said her mother was a wonderful cook. Purdy had doubts about that, but there was no way to ever know for sure. That food was gone, his grandmother was gone, her whole town was gone. Coal had come in and, according to his mother, "broke the heart of the land and scattered the family." The events of the day had put Purdy in a philosophical frame of mind. He decided that since the world was such a fragile place, where everything might be ruined at any moment, and the people you love can suddenly disappear, you might as well be nice. "It's good," he said.

"Really? You like it?"

"Yep. What is it?"

"What do you mean 'what is it?'" said Doreen. "It's spaghetti and meatballs, goofball."

"Yeah, I get that, but why is it crunchy?"

"Well, it's fried."

"Oh."

"Oh, and I didn't have meat so the meatballs are chicken nuggets, but they taste just like meatballs when they have the sauce on them, don't you think?"

"I do."

"Purdy, tell us what happened at the school," said Joe.

"But you know already," Purdy said.

"I got the Reader's Digest version from your mom, but I want to hear it all from you."

Purdy began reluctantly but warmed to the telling as he went along. Recollections that did not seem quite real seemed to solidify into fact when he put them into words. He told them everything that happened up to the point where he removed Simon from the classroom. "After I disappeared him I was really stuck. I didn't know what to do with the kid. He had seen me. He had seen Sockworld. How could I return him? At that point I was still pretty mad at him because I thought he was really there to shoot kids. I still feel angry sometimes. My hands fist up and my teeth grind when I think about it. The kids in that school were scared. I was scared. I seriously thought about leaving him up there."

"Why didn't you?" asked Joe.

"Well, I started thinking about you, and about the other people I've met in Sockworld. It just seemed too hard. I couldn't do it, no matter what he did. I couldn't... remember that guy we killed?"

"Sure."

"Whoa," said Doreen. "You make us sound like some mob family. Say it different."

"OK," said Purdy. "Remember that guy we, um, disintegrated?"

Doreen put her fingers on the bridge of her nose, the way she did when she had a headache. "Go on."

"Anyway, you didn't tell him he might get older, might die if he left Sockworld. After he blew away remember what I told you?"

"You said it wasn't my decision," said Joe.

"Right. It wasn't your decision. If I left that kid there... it just didn't seem like his future was my decision to make. It got me thinking about the other people in Sockworld too. I've been afraid to take them out because they could die, but I realized today – that's not my decision either. It should be their decision. I'm going to gather them up and let them decide for themselves if they want to stay or not."

"Darlin', that's wonderful," said Doreen.

"I knew you would think so," said Purdy. "Dad?"

"Of course, yes, it's the right thing to do."

"I was thinking Sunday," said Purdy, "when we go to the movies in Tucson. We could take them..."

"You want to take them to the movies?" said Joe.

Purdy groaned. "No, I meant take them to Tucson. Maybe not all of them will die. If some live they might be way old, so I thought I should take them out of Sockworld near a hospital. There's no hospital here."

"Oh," said Joe. "Good thinking. Sure, we can do that. So, you know that people in Sockworld can be hard to find. How are you going to gather them all up?"

"Don't worry," said Purdy. "I have connections."

<>

34

Up before the sun, Purdy rummaged through his top dresser drawer until he found the perfect white sock. He spread it out on his desk, took up a thick black marker, and began to write.

"Madame Bruneau, it is time. Gather above the church, Sunday, noon bell. Purdy"

After re-reading the message several times he added "(Mort)" in case Madame Bruneau had forgotten his name. He picked up the sock and disappeared though the roof. A huge moon was setting. It was almost as orange as the pumpkins that were decorating doorways all over town in anticipation of Halloween. The town was dimly illuminated. Purdy threw the sock into the sky and said, "Fly, my falcon." He watched as it drifted slowly north. After a minute, it was intercepted by a pair of dark socks, and the three drifted west toward the center of town.

When Purdy was allowed on the internet at school he began researching the closest hospitals, noting their addresses and looking at satellite views so he would recognize them from above. On Saturday he flew to Tucson to check them out. His plan was to appear his group behind a hospital, out of sight. He was looking for a hospital that had a back door with easy access to the emergency room, but no security camera. The security camera proved to be a deal breaker for all the hospitals on his list. He had never realized how many security cameras there were until he started looking for them. He would have to change his plan. His first thought was to disable the security cameras. That would be easy enough to do. Most perched on roof corners. He could throw a bag over them, or spray-paint the lenses, or snip a few wires. He concluded, however, that that would only send security guards rushing out to see what happened. If he couldn't disable the security cameras, perhaps he could disable the security guard who watched the monitors. That brought to mind a host of fun options.

He had been working on his speed. His father had bought him a baseball and glove. He played a couple of obligatory games of catch with his dad, which he found boring and pointless, but which he pretended to enjoy since his dad seemed to enjoy them. Afterwards, in an empty field, Purdy made catch more interesting for himself by throwing the ball as far as he could, and then appearing on the opposite side of the field to catch it. He believed that, with practice, he could pitch the ball, hit it, and then catch it all by himself. With his improved speed he was confident he could disappear a guard and then strand him on a rooftop, or up a tree, or down a laundry chute, all so fast the guard would never see him. He would love to hear that unfortunate guard's walkie-talkie message — *"Larry, this is Jim. I don't know how it happened, but I'm stuck up a tree. Do you copy? Hello?"*

The fact that security guards had radios or cell-phones killed the new plan. His simple plan was proving complicated. He was gaining, if not sympathy for modern criminals, then at least an appreciation of the difficulties they faced. As he hovered behind a hospital trying to figure out the security camera problem he was startled by the sight of a rat leaping out of a dumpster and vanishing into a hole in an adjacent fence. It had not occurred to him until then that the good people of Sockworld might not want to spend their last moments on Earth in a dark, dumpster-lined alley. A solution instantly presented itself. Several hospitals had small, adjoining park-like areas for the use of patients and visitors. He would appear his group beneath a security camera frustrating tree in one of these parks and then, if need be, he would transport survivors directly into the emergency room. Problem solved. He flew home.

His parents got in their car and left at 11:00 Sunday morning so they could meet him at San Gabriel's General Hospital in Tucson. Before they left, Joe took Purdy aside and said, "I know you have your mind set on doing this. Now don't get me wrong – it's a fine thing to do, but don't get your hopes up too much. I know those people… well, some of them. There's a good chance nobody will show up."

"I know," said Purdy.

"You know how upset you can get …"

"It's cool. Don't worry."

"You seem awfully confident. Wait," said Joe, "did you dream this?"

"No," said Purdy. "I just have a feeling about it."

"OK then."

"Good speech, though. Save it for the next time my hopes are about to get crushed. Happens all the time."

"Does it?"

"No, no, just joking. Exaggerating for comic effect. Don't worry about me."

"I do, though," said Joe. "That's my job. We'll talk about this later."

"See there," said Purdy, "I was hoping the conversation was over. Another hope crushed."

Too excited to wait for noon, Purdy flew to the church. The first Sockworldian to arrive was Richard, the young man he had met in the barber shop.

"Howdy," said Purdy.

"Uh, OK," said Richard. "They got a TV in this place?" He pointed to the church below them.

"No, I don't think so,"

"I'll go check."

"Wait," said Purdy. "Do you know if there are others coming?"

"Nah, they're waiting for the storm to pass."

"Storm? What storm? There's not a cloud in the…" Just then he saw a large black cloud to the south. "That's funny. I didn't see that before. Wait here." Purdy flew down and appeared on the roof of one of the church buildings. The cloud was not there. When he disappeared he saw it again. He had never imagined whole clouds might be caught in Sockworld. Joe had not mentioned it. He returned to Richard.

"Have you seen one of these storms before?" he asked.

"Oh, yeah," said Richard. "Happens all the time, like every ten years."

"Wow. Wait here. I'm going to check it out."

"No, don't go near it. It messes with your head."

"Don't worry," said Purdy, "nothing can hurt us here." He flew toward the storm, slowing as he got closer, no longer so certain it was harmless. Hovering directly beneath he saw the dark cloud was swirling rapidly clockwise. Every few minutes it would be lit up from inside by lightning, but, oddly, thunder never followed. Then, from out of the darkness, a giant dragon appeared.

35

The dragon looked exactly the way Purdy imagined a dragon would look. It was covered in shiny, reptilian scales. Its wings were black and leathery, like huge bat wings. Smoke billowed from its nostrils, and its eyes glowed red, like windows to some inner fire.

Purdy did not flee. He stayed still and watched with folded arms as the dragon flew in circles around him. It reared up in front of him.

"What?" said the dragon, "Not afraid?"

"Yeah, sorry," said Purdy. "It's just that, uh, nobody has been afraid of dragons since the middle ages, and even then I doubt they kept many people up nights worrying. Besides that, you're a biological impossibility. Animals are composed mostly of water, so how could a sack of water contain fire? And the wings, they're an extra set of limbs."

"A biological impossibility?" said the dragon. "Darn." It turned to smoke. When the smoke cleared there was a very old man in the dragon's place.

"You have to admit, it was an impressive display," said the man.

"It was." Although Purdy had never seen the man before he seemed very familiar. "I'm sorry, do I know you?"

"You should. Do you recall Socrates' famous dictum? 'Know thyself.'"

"Are we related?"

"In a sense," said the man. "I'm you eighty years from now."

Purdy instantly recognized himself in the man's saggy, wrinkled face. "No way," he said. "I'm not going to be fat."

"And you're basing that on what?" said old Purdy. "Your current diet of candy and junk food? Extrapolate your daily calorie count over eighty years. By rights, I should be the size of a small country."

"Shut up, I get it. Just because I eat that way now doesn't mean I always will. People eat different when they get older, like my mom..."

"Our mom," said old Purdy.

"Whatever. She ate road kill when she was a kid. She doesn't eat that now."

"Point taken. Our diet did change."

"I don't want to hear about it," said Purdy.

"But I'm sure you have lots of questions about the future. About your future."

Purdy thought about it. "I do. Of course I do, but I don't want to know. It's bad enough to live through something horrible. It would be a hundred times worse to have to dread it coming for years and years. I don't want to know anything."

"Not anything?"

"OK, just one thing. Will people drive flying cars eighty years from now?"

"No."

"Dang," said Purdy. "When is that ever going to happen? So, why are you here?"

"Why am I here."

"Why are you here?"

"Why am I here."

"Stop that," said Purdy.

"I was attempting to make a correction," said old Purdy. "As we are the same person, ask 'why am I here?'"

"Man, I never knew I was so annoying," said Purdy. "What I meant was, why a ninety-two year old me? Why not two year old me, or twenty year old me, or thirty, forty, fifty year old me? Why not a me convention?"

"It was supposed an old man's words would have more weight."

"So you are here to warn me about my weight?"

"No," said old Purdy, "but I am here to warn you…"

Just then Purdy heard screaming. He looked up and was amazed to see Savitri spinning along with the quickly spinning clouds.

"Purdy, help!" she screamed.

He was about to fly to her when old Purdy blocked his way.

"It's OK," said Purdy. "I've got this."

"She's not what I've come to warn you about. Your parents are about to be in an accident on the highway. You must go now."

"But Savitri…"

"You can't help everyone," said old Purdy. "You have to make a choice."

The words were familiar. Purdy thought, "Call me Sweetie Pie, call me Sweetie Pie."

"Purdy, help!" screamed Savitri. "Purdy! Sweetie Pie!"

"Sorry," Purdy shouted to her. "You'd never call me that. I have to let you go. You're not real."

Savitri vanished. Purdy had realized the cloud was indeed messing with his head, playing with his own thoughts and memories.

"I hope you won't say that to me," said old Purdy. "There's no telling which of us will disappear."

"I'll take our chances," said Purdy. "You're not real."

Old Purdy vanished. Purdy immediately moved to find his parents but found himself circling the cloud. Hard as he tried, he could not escape its pull. He looked down and saw birds flying far below, and further below, the desert. "Geronimo," he whispered, and appeared out of Sockworld. Instantly he was falling, the air buffeting him, a skydiver without a parachute. He spread his arms and legs and kept his eyes focused on the approaching ground. When he had fallen what he supposed was a sufficient distance from the cloud he disappeared again, and flew to the highway.

In seconds he spotted his mother's blue Chevy with its sun-scorched roof. He appeared in the back seat. "Get off the road!" he shouted.

"Purdy, you scared me," said Joe. "What are you doing here?"

"Get off… oh, heck!" He lunged over the seat, grabbed the steering wheel and turned it to the right. The car rumbled through the gravel by the side of the road and came to a stop in the desert.

"Purdy!" shouted Doreen. "Are you trying to kill…"

There was a loud bang, and the car that had been travelling alongside to their left blew a front tire. It swung wildly, first to the right, then to the left, and then straight to the right and into the desert ahead of them.

"It would have hit us," said Joe.

"Purdy, you saved our lives," said Doreen.

"But how did you know?" asked Joe.

"Something told me you were going to be in an accident," he said, skipping over a detailed account of his delusions in the cloud.

"But we weren't in an accident," said Joe. "This is huge. You changed the future."

"I guess I did." He smiled and enjoyed a moment of happiness before doubts crept in. They left the car and went to check on the other driver who they found shaken but not injured. Joe helped him change his tire, then they returned to their own car.

"If you're OK, I've got to get back," said Purdy.

"Of course, darlin'," said Doreen. "We'll see you at the hospital."

"OK, I'll see you there," said Purdy. "Weather permitting."

<>

36

A crowd had gathered above the church. Purdy counted eight men and five women, recognizing among them Madame Bruneau with her flowing cape. He wondered how so many Sockworld residents could have been unknown to him. Had they all come from Casi Nada, or had some travelled from far away to be here? What if every town and city has its own invisible population? The business of freeing people might never be over.

"You are late, as usual," said Madame Bruneau.

"Yes, sorry, I…"

"But we are glad you are here at last."

The group all stared at him expectantly, like the audience at a magic show. "Howdy, I'm Purdy," he began. "I don't know what Madame Bruneau has told you. I can, I mean I'm able to take you out of here, back to the real world, the world you came from, you know, with gravity and everything."

He had thought the statement from the short speech he had prepared would be met with some excitement, even cheering, but there was no reaction at all. The group continued to stare.

"Now you don't have to go," he continued, "but if you do…"

"We don't have to?" interrupted Richard.

"No, no, it's up to you."

"Good. There's a Gilligan's Island marathon on. Can't miss that." Richard flew off toward the barber shop. The rest of the group was becoming restless, and Purdy felt he was in danger of literally losing his audience.

"Anyway, as I was saying, if you do choose to leave here and go back to the real world you should know that time will catch up with you, really fast. You'll get older, and you may get so old, I mean you may be so old that you'll, that you'll, uh, die."

There was an immediate uproar.

"I thought we were dead," shouted a tall man.

"What?" said another, "we have to die again?"

"No, no," said Purdy. "You're not dead now."

"But I have no body," said the tall man. "How can we be alive with no body? You can have a body with no life, but not life with no body. Without a body you have nothing."

"And what of the soul, eh?" said Madame Bruneau. "Is that nothing to you? Just a plate of fish?"

A woman approached Purdy and said quietly, "If I owed money do I still owe it? And I had library books out."

"Moron, you have no body," the tall man shouted. "You can't survive without a body."

"You survived without a brain," the woman yelled back.

"Shut up!"

"Drop dead!"

"I am dead."

"Whoa, whoa," shouted Purdy. "Stop, I can explain." Despite his pleas, four members of the group flew off, still yelling at each other. The remaining group had been reduced to four men and four women. As there had been so great a misunderstanding regarding the physical state of potential returnees, Purdy decided a brief demonstration might be helpful. "Watch me, please," he said. He flew down and landed on the roof of one of the church buildings. He appeared and looked around. He picked up an empty beer can and drop kicked it, sending it clattering down the length of the roof. He disappeared into Sockworld again. The group closed in around him.

"What did it feel like?"

"Did you feel the sun on your face?"

"Was there a breeze?"

"Could you smell the beer?"

"Yes," said Purdy. "Yes to everything. It's life, just as you remember it, solid, and heavy, and painful sometimes, but real."

"I want to go," said a woman. "I want to go now."

"Me too," said another.

"Take me," said a third.

"I'll take everyone who wants to go," said Purdy, "but I need to know you understand that if you are too old you'll only survive a few seconds before turning to dust. You need to think about it a few minutes."

"I have waited for years," said Madame Bruneau. "I am ready."

"What's there to think about?" said a man. "My family is dead. My dog is dead. Strangers are living in my house. The world has grown wild and crowded, like a garden gone to seed. There is no place for me. I'd rather turn to dust than live as a shadow among strangers."

"A moment to feel the breeze in my hair and solid ground beneath my feet," said a woman, "would be enough."

"Good," said Purdy. "The rest of you please just take a minute." It was then that he noticed a woman standing apart from the group. He supposed she had just arrived. She was wearing a long grey dress and as he approached Purdy noticed her image seemed to shimmer more than the others. "Hello," he said.

"Hello," she repeated.

"Did you hear what I was saying?"

The woman nodded. As he talked to her, it seemed to Purdy that her hair and eye color kept changing, but he found himself unable to recall what color it had been a moment before.

"I can take you out of here," said Purdy. "Will you come with me?"

"Will you come with me?" repeated the woman.

"I'm sorry," said Purdy. "Do you speak English? Se habla…"

"I understand," said the woman.

"OK, so will you come with us?"

"There is another door," said the woman.

"Yes, I've heard that, but I've looked everywhere and never seen it. Where is it?"

"Where would you like it to be?"

"What? Wait, it moves?" asked Purdy.

"No, you move."

"I'm confused. Go back, un-say, start over."

"Hello," said the woman.

"OK, not that far back. There's a door. How do I find it? What does it look like?"

"You will not find it by looking."

"Good to know," said Purdy. "How, then?"

"How did you find this world?"

"So, it's a feeling?"

The woman nodded. "Your powers are not fully realized. You will find it eventually."

"And what's on the other side of that door?"

The woman looked up. Purdy followed her gaze and saw the little dove he had seen before floating down towards him. He put up his hands and caught it. "Look," he said, but the woman was gone.

<>

37

The bird settled itself into Purdy's hands and fell asleep again. Purdy tucked it into his shirt and moved back to the group.

"If you're done talking to yourself," said Madame Bruneau, "We are ready."

"All of you? OK, great. I'm going to bring you out of here, but not here. We should be near a hospital. If you do survive, you may need medical care. It's just a little trip, OK? Everybody ready? Follow me."

Purdy led them along the familiar route above the highway, flying out in front, the lead goose of a very ungainly looking flock. He kept the pace slow, flying only a little faster than the cars below. He knew that for many, if not all of his group, it would be their last view of the harsh, beautiful landscape below. Soon the cacti gave way to houses, billboards, gas stations, factories, and tall office buildings. He stopped the group above the hospital.

"Well, here we are," he said. "You can still change your minds. No? OK, I'm just going to go down and make sure the coast is clear. You can use this time to say prayers, or whatever."

Purdy flew down and found his parents sitting on a bench below the tree he had chosen, but he was dismayed to find a couple of strangers seated on an opposing bench. "Hey, Joe."

"Hey. Everything OK?"

"Purdy, I can hear you," said Doreen.

"You can?"

"Yep. I always wondered why only your Daddy could hear you. It didn't seem fair. Now you're coming in loud and clear. This is so cool."

"That's great, Mom," said Purdy.

"Guess you ain't such hot stuff now," she said to her husband.

"How did it go?" asked Joe.

"OK," said Purdy. "I've got eight people with me. Do you think you can get rid of those other guys?"

"Leave it to me, son," said Joe. He began coughing.

"You poor dear," said Doreen.

"Darling, you really shouldn't be sitting so close," Joe said loudly between coughs. "It's highly contagious."

Doreen put her hand over her mouth and nose. "You poor dear. And they say you only have a week to live?"

"Maybe less."

The couple across from them got up and walked quickly into the hospital.

"Thanks," said Purdy. "See you in a minute." He returned to his group.   "Is everyone ready?"

"Just a moment," said Madame Bruneau. She removed her cape of socks and tossed it up. It burst into a thousand socks and hovered in a cloud above her. "Go," she said. "I am done."

The socks wavered back and forth above the group, then started moving toward Purdy, trying to form a cape around his shoulders. Purdy brushed them away. "No," he said. "No, it's OK. You're free." With that, the socks rose up in a spinning column and then burst apart, flying away in all directions.

"Well," he said, "if we're done with the laundry, what do you say we go home? Let's see, I've never done more than one person before. I think if we join hands in a circle that should work." All nine clitched hands together and floated slowly down to the ground beneath the tree. Purdy then brought them into the real world. Most fell to the ground, having grown unused to the press of grav-ity. Joe and Doreen rushed in to help them to their feet. Purdy took Madame Bruneau's hand and arm and helped her up.

"Merci," she said. She was rapidly aging, her back bending, hair whiten-ing and thinning, showing patches of scalp. She took hold of his hands. "Merci, merci."

"My pleasure," said Purdy. "Je vous en prie."

"Ah, tres bien," she said, and fell into dust.

All around him, men and women were disappearing. Doreen shrieked when a woman she had been supporting went to dust in her arms. When the dust settled, two women and one man from the group were left, ancient but alive. Purdy felt a fluttering near his heart, reached in his shirt and pulled out the dove. The old people tottered toward him, and he held out the bird so they could pet its small head.

"It's beautiful," said Doreen. "You gonna keep it?"

"No, I shouldn't." Purdy lifted his hands up and uncapped them. The dove flapped its wings tentatively, then flew up into the tree. "Mom, do you have a tissue? I've got bird poop on my hand."

The elders began trying to walk around, with various degrees of success. One old woman stumbled out of the shade, turned her face up to the sun, and smiled. Another turned in tight circles, clapping her hands, alternatively shout-ing, "Hallelujah," and "I'm cold." For the old man, each step appeared painful, and was accompanied by a moan which sounded like whale song heard through the side of a creaking ship.

"Purdy, maybe it's time you take them inside," said Joe.

"Yeah, I guess."

They rounded the elders up and each received hugs and handshakes from Purdy and his parents. Purdy then joined hands with them again and dis-appeared them. They floated through the halls of the hospital. Purdy found an empty curtained exam space in the emergency room, and appeared them again.

"I've got to leave you now," said Purdy. "You'll be taken care of here. It's probably best you don't mention my name."

"What's your name?" said the old man.

"Perfect," said Purdy. "Good-bye." He disappeared, but watched to make sure they'd be found. After a few minutes a nurse pulled the curtain aside. The three elders were sitting on the bed.

"Who is the patient here?" the nurse snapped.

The three old people looked at each other, then they all raised their hands. Purdy returned to his parents beneath the tree and found them stooped over, brushing the dust with branches.

"What are you doing?" he asked.

"Look what we found," said Joe, holding out a handful of rings, bracelets, and coins. "This can be a real money maker."

"It's gross," said Purdy. "No."

"We'll put the money in your college fund," said Joe.

"I don't want my tuition paid for by grave robbing."

"It's only technically…"

"Stop, Joe," said Doreen. "Can't you see he's upset? Darlin', are you OK?"

"I guess," said Purdy. "It's just… so many people… just gone."

"I know, but you done them a kindness. You did. They were suffering where they were. They made their choice, and now they're at peace. You sent them to a better place."

"I wish I could believe that," said Purdy.

Joe clapped his arm around Purdy's back and said proudly, "My son, the angel of death."

<>

38

After the family washed the dust of dead people off their hands they had lunch at a fast-food restaurant, then caught the latest zombie movie.

"What did you think?" said Joe on the ride home.

"There wasn't enough blood," said Doreen.

"Are you kidding?" said Purdy. "There was way too much blood."

"How do you figure?"

"Zombies are dead, right? When you're dead your blood settles and co-agulates. So, when you blow a zombie's head off there should be little or no blood."

"You're missing the point," said Joe. "Zombies are a commentary on the greedy, thoughtless way people live today."

"Don't embarrass yourself, darlin'." said Doreen. "We're talking about real zombies."

Once back in town, Joe veered off the usual route home.

"Where are we going?" said Purdy.

"I just have to make a quick stop," said Joe. The car stopped in front of a bright green house in Savitri's neighborhood. "I'll be right back."

Purdy watched as his father knocked on the door, shook hands with a man, and went inside. He emerged ten minutes later carrying a large cardboard box. "Open up," he said, and Purdy opened his door. Joe placed the box on his son's lap and said, "It's for you."

Inside the box sat a chubby brown and white puppy. "Oh, wow!" Purdy exclaimed. He picked it up and the puppy sleepily licked him on the nose.

"It's so cute," said Doreen.

"Fellow at work was trying to get rid of some puppies," said Joe. "I had him save me the last puppy. A boy should have a dog."

"Is it OK, Mom?"

"Course it is," she said. "It's so sweet. Let me see."

Purdy handed the dog to her.

"Do you like it?" said Joe, getting back in the car.

"I love it. Thank you so much," Purdy said. "I'll take real good care of it. Let's see, we'll need puppy food, and a collar and a leash, and a litter box, and toys, and…"

"A litter box?" said Doreen. "It's a dog."

"I'll explain later," said Joe.

"What kind is it?" Purdy asked.

"Its pedigree is pure mutt."

"Did you know about this, Mom?"

"Sure did," she said. "I knew you'd like it, and I thought it would be nice for the puppy and the baby to grow up together."

"What baby?" Purdy looked back and forth at his parents. "Oh my gosh! How did that happen? No, I don't want to know, I mean… Oh my gosh!"

"You're going to be a big brother," said Doreen.

Purdy sat back.

"What's the matter," said Doreen. "Aren't you excited?"

"Sure I am."

"What is it?" asked Joe.

"What if it's like me?" Purdy said.

"Well, huh, hadn't thought about that," said Joe. "I'm sure that would be a very nice thing. You'll be there to teach it."

"But what if it's not like me?" Purdy said. "What if it's, you know, normal?" He looked to his mom.

"Oh, hell," she said, "guess we'll love it anyway."

Purdy laughed until tears filled his eyes.

<>

In early November Purdy was in front of his home, trying to train his dog. "Sit," he commanded. The puppy barked. "Not speak, sit!" His father came down the stairs.

"Joe, watch this," said Purdy. "Cloud, speak!" The dog sat down and scratched its ear.

"Don't expect too much," said Joe. "It has a brain the size of a walnut." "Just wait. I'll teach it."

"Purdy, do you know anything about this?" Joe tapped the front page of the newspaper.

"About what?"

"Let me read you something." Joe read:

"It's not unusual to see ghosts and goblins on Halloween. This past Halloween, however, several Casi Nada residents reported seeing a 'real' ghost.

"I just thought it was a kid wearing a sheet," recalled Ms Rebecca Sandoval, "but after I put some candy in the ghost's bag it stepped back, said 'Boo!' and disappeared. I was so scared I dropped the bowl of candy."

""Well?" said Joe.

"Ghosts," said Purdy. "No, doesn't make sense. Like there are invisible people flying around. Some people will believe anything."

The invisible woman nodded.

<>

$\mathbf{T}$he President was sitting up in bed reading a Western. After a while his eyes began to droop, so he put the book down on his nightstand and clapped his hands. The light went out.

Clap. The light went on. A masked figure stood at the foot of the bed.

"Who are you?" said the President. "How did you…?"

"I mean you no harm," the masked man said. "I can explain everything. Just please don't push that…"

The President pushed the button. A team of Secret Service agents burst through the door. Two agents grabbed the President under the arms and dragged him from the room. The other two went around the room, poking their guns into every nook and cranny. They found nothing.

After an hour, the President decided he must have been dreaming, though behind his back a Secret Service agent made a gesture suggesting he must have been drinking. The President returned to bed, and after looking around nervously, clapped his hands. The light went out.

Clap. The light went on. "Mr. President, I mean you no harm," said the masked man at the foot of the bed. "Just hear me out. As I've proved, I have the ability to get in and out of places without being seen. I believe I can help you with the hostage situation in Olliestan."

"But, who are you?"

"They call me…" The masked man made a particularly rude noise. "… Captain Gas."

Clap.

<>-<>-<>

About the Author

Cary Grossman was born at an early age in a log cabin in Brooklyn, New York. He has lived most of his life, however, in Arizona, which is much like New York in that they are both states. Cary demonstrated an early aptitude for choosing careers that would keep him poor and humble by deciding to become a cartoonist. He did, in fact, become one, and had some success selling to the country's top magazines. What he did not realize was that the golden age of magazine cartooning was coming to an end. It was rather like deciding to become a sailor and signing on to be a crew member on the Titanic. In another brilliant economic move Cary studied painting in college. Deciding "why have two non-profit careers when I can have three?" he also became a writer. He received a fellowship to work at the MacDowell Colony, where he wrote his first novel which – wait for it – was never published. His short stories, however, have appeared in a number of literary journals. Now his novel, "Sockworld," has sprung upon the eager reading public. If you are a fan of rags-to-riches stories you can help by buying a copy for yourself, and 10,000 copies for friends and family.